"Sallis writes crime novels that read like literature."
—*Los Angeles Times*

"Classic American crime of the highest order."
—*Time Out*

"Sallis is an unsung genius of crime writing."
—*Independent on Sunday*

"James Sallis is a superb writer." —*Times*

"[A] master of American noir . . . Sallis creates vivid images in very few words and his taut, pared down prose is distinctive and powerful." —*Sunday Telegraph*

"Sallis' spare, concrete prose achieves the level of poetry."
—*Telegraph*

"Sallis is a wonderful writer, dark, lyrical and compelling."
—*Spectator*

"Sallis is a fastidious man, intelligent and widely read. There's nothing slapdash or merely strategic about his work." —*London Review of Books*

"Carefully crafted, restrained and eloquent."
—*Times Literary Supplement*

"James Sallis is without doubt the most underrated novelist currently working in America." —*Catholic Herald*

The
Long-Legged
Fly

Books by James Sallis

The Long-Legged Fly

James Sallis

This edition first published in 2019 by
Soho Press, Inc.
853 Broadway
New York, NY 10003

Library of Congress Cataloging-in-Publication Data

Sallis, James
The long-legged fly / James Sallis.
Series: Lew Griffin series |
First published in 1992 by No Exit Press.

ISBN 978-1-64129-143-9
eISBN 978-1-64129-144-6

1. Missing persons—Fiction. 2. Mystery fiction.
PS3569.A462 L66 2019 813'.54—dc23 2019016064

Interior art: © Bodor Tivadar/Shutterstock
Interior design: Janine Agro

Printed in the United States of America

10 9 8 7 6 5 4 3 2 1

To
Karyn

The
Long-Legged
Fly

Part One 1964

Chapter One

"Hello, Harry."

His sick eyes slid in the light. He was wearing a corduroy coat over a denim shirt, chinos bagged out at knee and butt, pant legs too long, cuffs frayed. They'd all seen better days, clothes and man alike. Harry had always been a sharp dresser, people said; they even used the word natty. But now skag and his own errant heart had got him.

"Carl?" His voice was an emphysematous whisper. Even now a cigarette dangled out the side of his mouth. It waggled up and down as he talked. "I got the money, man. Business as usual, right? Just like you said." A rumbling cough deep in his chest.

"No rush, Harry. Be cool, there's plenty of time. Let up a little, enjoy life." The yard lights were behind me and he squinted at the shadow moving toward him. Not that it would have made much difference. He didn't know me from Earl Long. "And anyhow, first I want to tell you a story. You like stories, Harry?"

Behind us, oil derricks heaved and rested, heaved and rested.

"Magazine Street. Ten-fifteen, Saturday night, about a month ago. There was a girl from Mississippi, Harry. And a party. And you. Any of this beginning to sound familiar?"

His eyes searched the darkness around him.

"I've been looking for you a long time, Harry. It took a long time to find you. A man like you, with your needs, he shouldn't be so hard to find."

He took the cigarette out of his mouth and threw it down. It lay there like a half-blind eye. I stepped out of the light and when he saw me he was scared for the first time, really scared. Old fears die hard.

"It's only a story, of course. Stories help us go on living. Stories can't hurt anyone, can they, Harry?"

I let him see the knife in my hand then, a leatherworker's knife.

"Big Black Sambo's coming to get you, Harry. Nigger's gonna carve you up like you did her. Nothing left for the pigs and chickens, not even enough for soul food."

His eyes moved. He knew escape was somewhere. But he also knew that like everything else in his life it was going to get away from him.

"Look, man, I don't know who you are, but you got it all wrong. You listen to me, it wasn't my fault. I just fix things—arrange them, like—that's all I ever done. It was those crazies, man. Goddamn long hair and kraut van. They're the ones did that girl."

It tumbled out of him much as the world must have

gone in: fitful starts, none of them connected; and under-neath, everything blurring together.

I raised the knife and light glinted on the curved blade.

"Yeah, I know, Harry. Crazies on skag and smack feeding new monkeys, crazies on speed and booze and horse and the rush of a couple hundred dollars they just boosted out of some mom and pop's till. But who got the stuff for them, Harry? Who gave it to them and started the party? How much of their stake did it cost them? And whose idea to bring the girl into that?"

Fear lit his eyes like a torch. All around us oil derricks sighed, the last breaths of tired old men.

He turned to run but fear tangled his legs. He fell. I let him crawl, a few yards. He was sobbing. Choking.

"You didn't even know her name, Harry." I walked up slowly behind him, got a foot under and flipped him over. He flopped like something not human, and his eyes rolled. I let him have a good long look at my face, all the things that were in it.

"Sleepy after your bedtime story?"

Blood welled out of his throat and soaked denim, cor-duroy, ground. No light left behind those eyes now. No light anywhere.

I searched his pockets and got the money—that was for the kid. Then I bent down and opened up his wasted belly with the knife.

"That was for Angie," I said.

Behind us, oil derricks shushed any eulogy.

Chapter Two

I HADN'T BEEN to the apartment in three days, the office in four, so it was a toss-up. Finally, cruising down St. Charles, I decided the office was closer so what the hell. I went around the block a few times. All the parking spaces were filled. I finally pulled the Cad into a towaway zone and raised the hood. Weak, but it might work. It had before.

The bakery was doing hot business, but upstairs it looked like everybody had moved out. There was something peculiar about that at two-fifteen in the afternoon. Then I remembered it was Labor Day. Maybe I'd have to do some work to celebrate.

I stopped in front of the door marked "Lewis Griffin, In estigations" (the *v* had escaped a year or so back; most days I envied it) and got out the key. There were a lot of notes tacked to the door—I had an informal arrangement with the bakery for taking messages. I ripped them off, turned the key and went on inside. The floor was littered with mail they'd dropped through the slot. I scooped it up and dropped it on the desk with the messages.

There was a half-filled glass of bourbon and an almost empty bottle on the desk. A fly floated in what was left in the glass. I thought about it, fished the fly out with a letter-opener, drank, poured in the rest of the bottle. Then I sat down to go through all the junk.

Most of it was just that. Circulars, subscription renewal notices, religious pamphlets. There were three letters from the bank that I was overdrawn and would I please at my earliest convenience drop by and see Mr. Whitney. There was also a telegram. I held it up, turning it over and over in my hands. Never liked those things.

I finally ripped it open and looked. There was the usual salad of numbers and letters that meant nothing. Under that was the message.

FATHER GRAVELY ILL STOP ASKING FOR YOU STOP
BAPTIST MEMORIAL MEMPHIS STOP PLEASE CALL
STOP LOVE MOTHER

I sat there staring at the yellow paper. Ten minutes must have gone by. The old man and I had never been close, not for a long time anyhow, but now he was asking for me. Or was that just something Mom put in? And what the hell happened, anyhow? I couldn't see anything short of a train or howitzer ever stopping the old horse.

I got up and went to the window, taking the bourbon with me. I put it down in one gulp and put the glass on the sill. Down in the street a group of kids were playing what looked like cops and robbers. The robbers were winning.

I went back to the desk and dialed LaVerne's number. I didn't really expect to catch her this time of day, but she got it on the third ring.

"Lew? Listen, man, I've been trying to get in touch with you all week. Your mother's been calling me two, three times a day. I left messages all over this town."

"Yeah, I know, honey. Sorry. I've been away on business."

"But you always let me know . . ."

"Didn't know myself until the last minute." I looked wistfully at the empty bottle on the desk (good word, wistfully), wondering if the drug-store across the street would be open. I hadn't noticed. "But I'm back now and looking to see you."

"What is it, Lew? What's wrong?"

"Mom didn't say?"

"She wouldn't even have told me who she was if she didn't need something."

"My father's sick. I don't know, a heart attack, a stroke, maybe an accident—something, anyhow. 'Gravely ill' was what she said."

"Lew. You've gotta go up there. Next plane."

"And what would I use for money?"

She paused. "I've got money."

"Like the man says, Thanks but no thanks."

Another pause. "Someday that pride of yours'll kill you, Lew. The pride or the anger, I don't know which'll get you first. But look, it can be a loan, okay?"

"Forget it, Verne. Besides, I'm on a case." I was

beginning to wonder why I had called her in the first place. But who else was there? "I'll call tonight, find out what's happening. And I'll be in touch tomorrow. Hang in there."

"You too, Lew. You know where to find me. Bye."

"Yeah."

I put the receiver down and looked again at the empty bottle. Maybe Joe's was the place for me tonight. I looked at my watch. Maybe eight, nine would be the best time to call. Maybe they'd know something by then. Maybe they knew something already.

I threw the letters from the bank in the waste-basket and headed out the door.

When I got to the street, my car was gone.

Chapter Three

AFTER BAILING THE car out down by the river—$47.50; they required cash but I managed to hang some bad paper on them; they also required that I affix the new 1964 license plate I'd been carrying in the back seat before I left the lot—I drove to Joe's.

It's off Decatur, but you won't find it if you don't know where to look. The barmaids are all pros; they migrated from bar to bar all through the downtown area before they found their way to Joe's and settled in here, like old folks retiring to Florida.

I sat down at the bar and Betty brought me a double bourbon. I sat there smoking and putting down drink after drink. The ashtray was full and the bottle Betty was pouring out of was going down fast when Joe came in. He wanted to know what the Saints' chances were. I told him. He said ain't it the truth.

Several working girls came in, gave me a quick eye and moved along. Betty told me about the latest problems with getting to see her kids.

"What else's going on?" I asked her at one point.

"Tryin' to stay out of trouble but people won't let me," she said.

That's about the size of it, I thought.

At nine I walked over to the corner phone and placed a call to Baptist Hospital in Memphis, person-to-person for Mrs. Arthur Griffin, charging it to the office. I was routed through several operators and finally got a man who said, "Fifth-floor intensive care."

"Mrs. Arthur Griffin," the operator said.

"Just a minute. She may be with her husband; I'll check."

The phone was quiet for some minutes. I watched them meander past like sheep on Joe's revolving Schlitz clock above the bar. Finally a voice came on.

"Lewis? Lewis, is that you?"

"Go ahead," the operator said.

"Mom. Listen, what's going on?"

"It's bad, Lewis. Where have you been? I been tryin' to get you all week long. It's bad. It's a heart attack, Lewis. He's had a heart attack. A bad one, the doctors say. Now let me get this right." She was probably reading it off a piece of paper. "A myocardial infarction."

Somehow I'd known. "How's he doing?"

"Holding his own, Lewis, holding his own. They say the crisis comes in three days. If he passes that three days, then his chances get a lot better."

We had a bad connection. I could hear other, distant voices in the wires.

"Mom, listen, is there anything I can do? Anything at all?"

"Just he's askin' for you, Lewis. He wants to see his only boy. Lewis, he knows. He knows he's dyin'. He wants to see you before that comes."

Betty motioned from the bar, wanting to know if I wanted another one. I nodded.

"I can't make it, Mom. Not now. I'm on a case. But if there's anything I can do, anything at all . . ." I left the rest unsaid. Of course there was nothing I could do. I had a feeling there was nothing anyone could do. Far back in the wires I heard someone say, "Well, then, Harold, when *are* you coming home?"

Betty brought the new drink around to me at the phone and I had a long draw off it. It went down like a wire brush.

"Lewis, you've got to come."

"I can't, Mom. The case might break any day. I've got to be here. But I'll call—I'll be in touch. You keep me posted."

"They're taking him to surgery tomorrow, Lewis. They're going to put some kind of a balloon in his heart, something that's supposed to help him. I hoped you'd be here."

"I can't. I just can't. Not now. But I'll be in touch."

"Let me give you this number," she said. "There's always someone here. You make friends fast when something like this happens. It's one of the waiting rooms. We all sleep here at night. Everybody looks out for each other. Now you call, you hear? I never can get you."

She read off the number and I copied it down in my notebook, scrawling underneath it: Dad. Someone on the line was saying, "But I can't wait that long, I gotta know tomorrow."

"I'll be talking to you then, Mom," I said, and hung up.

I went over to the bar and had three straight doubles. How many of these was it that had killed Dylan Thomas? Then I scooped up my change, all but a couple of dollars, and moved on.

Chapter Four

"Roaches," I told the bartender at a hole-in-the-wall in the Irish Channel. His name was sewn over his shirt pocket, PAT, but whoever did the needlework, in cursive, left a heavy line trailing from the belly of the P to the A, so it looked more like RAT.

In a notoriously wild city, the Channel at one time and for a long time was the wildest spot of all, scene of bars with names like Bucket of Blood, showers of bricks for encroaching outsiders, police killings. Whenever it rained, which in New Orleans was damn near always, water poured down from the Garden District just uptown onto the poor, low-living Irish here, which is probably where the name came from.

"Forget the Longs and political machines, forget the Mafia, the Petroleum Club, the Church or city hall: *roaches* are the ones who *really* run New Orleans. Our proudest product, our veritable *raison d'être. No* one does roaches like we do. Ought to be a statue of one out there on the river where everybody could see it, big as a building.

"Other people's roaches, other *place*'s roaches, run for cover when you turn the lights on. You ever seen any different? But not here, man. New Orleans roaches are more liable to drop to one knee and give out with a chorus or two of 'Swanee.' *They're* the true Negroes, roaches are, the only pure strain that's left, maybe. You *know* what happened in all them woodpiles.

"And the damn things've been around forever. You've got fossils that are two hundred and fifty thousand goddam years old and the roaches in there are exactly like the ones we could go pull out of your bathroom over there right now. They don't *have* to change, man; they can live off of anything. Or nothing.

"Whatever we dream up to kill them, they learn to live off it. One of them can live for a month off the glue on a postage stamp, for godsake. Cut off their heads and they go on living, even—only finally they starve to death.

"And here's something else. Found this in a book published at least a hundred years ago. This was like the Raid of its day, what everybody did. You were supposed to write the roaches a letter, this book says, and you'd say something like, 'Hey, Roaches, you've been on my case long enough, guys, so now it's time to go bother my neighbors, right?' Then you'd put this letter wherever the buggers were swarming. But first you've got to fold the letter and seal it and go through all the usual shit, the writer says. Like the roaches are gonna know if you get it wrong, if you don't put on enough postage or whatever. And then he tells you: 'It is well, too, to write legibly and punctuate according to rule.'"

"You're drunk, mister," the barkeep said.

"I am most assuredly that very thing," I said with the best Irish lilt I could manage. Just talking was hard enough at that point. "It's been a long siege."

"Have to cut you off, buddy. Sorry."

"No problem. I was cut off a long time ago. If you only knew." I pointed more or less at the stitching on his shirt. "You Irish?"

"Hell no. Named for my mother, Patricia: Pat." Then, with a grin: "You?"

"It's converted this last St. Pat's Day I was. Hopin' just a bit of the luck-of-the might rub off?"

"And has it?"

"Not so much as a smudge, I'm sorry to tell you. Not a smudge."

And scuttled home in the darkness.

Chapter Five

A CASE—THAT'S WHAT I'd told Mom and Verne both. But the case had holes you could drive a transport truck through and the break I'd mentioned was as far away as the end of Pinocchio's nose on Liar's Day. I thought about the kids playing cops and robbers down by the office. Was that all I was doing?

I mixed a cup of instant, poured in bourbon, and stretched out on the swayback couch in my half of a shotgun house on Dryades. It was five in the morning. My tongue felt like someone's dirty glove. Little men with jackhammers and earth-moving machinery were rebuilding the inside of my head.

For me it had begun two weeks ago in Joe's. I had turned an errant husband over to his wife in time for lunch and come there to spend the check. That's how big it was.

At that time of day, Joe's was filled with Greek sailors and the kind of working girls who hustle day and night just to break even. There were a few scattered businessmen off Canal Street—after all, the place is an institution—and over in the corner, an old man with things bent all around his wrists, neck and ankles. They looked like old spoons, bits of copper wire, just about anything you'd pick up off the street. He was drinking bottled Dixie. He had a scraggly, filthy beard and hair that crept out like vines from beneath a wool knit cap. The place also had more than the usual number of flies, brought there by Joe's free lunch, which consists of hard-boiled eggs (heavy on the *hard*) and chopped ham sandwiches out of a can.

I was halfway through my third Jax, sitting alone at one end of the bar, when I looked up and saw these two dudes walk in. Both wore modified military attire, fatigues and caps, with black high-top tennis shoes. One was deep, ebony black, the other coffee-colored. *Café au lait*.

They looked the place over, then went to the far end of the bar and said something to Bobbie. She waved a hand my way and they followed the hand.

"Lewis Griffin?" the black one said.

I held up my hand for another Jax. Bobbie nodded.

"Buy you fellows something?"

"We don't pollute our bodies with spirits," *Café au Lait* told me.

"Mr. Griffin," the black one said, "we are in need of your professional services."

Bobbie brought the beer and I slid a dollar across the bar toward her.

"Sit down?" I said.

"We'll stand." I was sure they knew where the back door was, too.

"Have it your way." Bobbie brought change. "Now, what is it that I can do for you?"

"It's a matter of some discretion." The black one seemed to be a natural leader. He looked around the bar. "We would prefer to speak in less public a place."

"It's here or nowhere," I said. Never give a client the advantage; he'll think he owns you. Besides, I was thirsty.

"We have been looking for you for three days," Blackie said. "Your office, your apartment. A man in your business should make himself more easily available."

"Those who need me usually find me, sooner or later."

"I suppose we are proof of that statement, yes?" So *Café au Lait* hadn't lost his tongue after all.

"As I say, it's a matter of some discretion. Your name has come to us from mutual friends. And it's a matter which only a brother could handle."

That "brother" should have warned me; I should have got up then and left. And if we had any mutual friends, I'd turn in an honest tax report next year.

"You've heard, of course, of Corene Davis?" Blackie said. At mention of her name, *Café au Lait* raised his open hand to chest level, then closed it. The old man with the spoons looked our direction and snorted. I knew how he felt.

"I subscribe to *Time* like everybody else," I said.

"We—by which I mean, our group—we had arranged a speaking engagement for her here in New Orleans. It was a matter of considerable dispute, as you may realize. A black leader, and a black woman what's more, in the deepest South." He looked around the bar again. The three of us were the only black faces in it. I suppose that proved something to him. "Many of her supporters thought it was foolish."

Bobbie brought me another beer. Maybe she figured I needed it.

"At any rate," Blackie went on, "it was to have been at the Municipal Auditorium, the eighteenth of August, at eight P.M. She was coming in early that morning to speak to some student groups at Tulane and Loyola. She did that wherever she went. Spoke to students, I mean."

"The force of the future," *Café au Lait* added. I looked at his hand. It remained still.

"At ten-fifteen on the night of the seventeenth," Blackie continued, "Corene Davis boarded a night flight to New Orleans at Idlewild. It was a nonstop flight, and a number of her supporters saw her aboard. When we met her plane here in New Orleans—we are a local group, you understand—she was not aboard. Nor has she been heard from since."

"And you fear . . ."

"That she has been kidnapped."

"Or worse," *Au Lait* added.

"She has many enemies among the establishment," Blackie said. "Surely you can understand that."

"I can indeed. But you need the police, not me."

The two looked at one another.

"It's a joke," *Au Lait* finally said.

Blackie looked back at me. "Surely you know that nothing good can come of that, Mr. Griffin."

"Yeah. Yeah, I guess I do." I finished the Jax in front of me and signaled Bobbie for another one. "Just what is it you expect from me?"

"We expect you to *find* her, man."

"Or find out what's happened to her," *Au Lait* said.

"I see. Has there been a ransom note, anything like that?"

"There's been nothing, man. And lots of it."

"And you haven't released this to the press, the police. How did you explain her missing the engagement?"

"We covered, friend, we covered." I suspected Blackie didn't like me a hell of a lot. "No one knows about this but our people in New York, and us. And now you."

"Maybe she doesn't want to be found—you consider that?"

"Corene? She was devoted, Griffin. Righteous."

I shrugged. "Just a thought. Okay, I'll give it a look. I'll need some information from you." I got out my notebook and took down the flight number, departure and arrival times. "She ever been to New Orleans before?"

He shook his head. "What do you want to know that for?"

"People tend to repeat themselves. They'll stay where they've stayed before, eat the same kind of foods. But mostly I'm just trying to get the feel of the thing. Her habits, hobbies, things she liked."

"Her work was her life."

"Right on," *Au Lait* said.

The businessmen had drifted out the door, along with

several sailors and some of the girls. Their places had been taken by a pimp in a yellow suit and two guys who looked like narcs. The old man with the spoons and things had gone to sleep with his head back against the wall. Flies were dipping wings over his open mouth.

"I'll be in touch," I said. "How do I find you?"

Blackie looked at *Au Lait*, back at me. Then he rattled off an address and phone number. "I'm never there, though. Leave a message."

I copied them down in the notebook, writing at the top of the page: Corene Davis.

"That all you need?" Blackie said.

"I get fifty a day and expenses, no questions asked. Two days up front. Any problem with that?"

"None." Blackie handed over a hundred-dollar bill that looked as though it had been folded tightly into someone's watch pocket and sent through the washer a few times.

They walked to the door and damned if they didn't turn around together at the last minute and, raising their hands to chest level, close them into fists. It looked like it was choreographed. Then they went out the door. Damned if *I* know how they'd lived this long. If the cops don't get you, the crackers will.

But anyhow, I had a case.

Power to the people.

Chapter Six

THE FIRST THING I'd done when I got back to the office—there was the usual accumulation of mail and messages—was clip a recent picture of Corene Davis from a copy of *Time*. Then I put in a call to United at Idlewild, finally got through, and was informed that, yes, Miss Corene Davis had had a coach reservation on Flight 417 for New Orleans. She had boarded shortly before takeoff, seat 15-A. The man I talked to remembered her, her being so famous and all. He'd been working the desk that day. She had two pieces of luggage. He gave me the name of the captain and stewardesses on the flight. I thanked him and hung up.

I sat there for a while watching twilight seep up around everything. The sky had a red tint to it, and everything smelled of magnolia and the river.

Finally I called downtown and asked for Sergeant Walsh. After a long wait, he came on.

"Don? Lew," I said. "I want to drop a name on you. Corene Davis."

"That bitch." There was a long pause. "You know I had half this force turned out for security—you'd have thought the president was coming to town. And what happens? The broad doesn't show." Walsh turned away from the phone for a moment, said something, was back. "Why?"

I wasn't sure how much I could tell him. Dissembling had kept us alive and more or less intact for a long time when nothing else could.

"I'd been looking forward to hearing her talk," I said after a moment. "Wondering what happened."

"Great. I've got fourteen unsolved homicides, the makings of a race riot out in Gentilly of all places, the commissioner and assorted councilmen on my tail like a hive of bees—big, hairy, *mad* bees—and you call up to chat about some trouble-making yankee bitch nigger."

"Then I guess you better get to work," I said. "But you know, Don, these days that kind of talk's a little . . . passé, if you know what I'm saying."

A pause. "Okay, Lew. So she ain't no bitch."

"Knew you'd see it my way."

"Sorry. Bad day. So what'd'ya need?"

"Just what happened."

"Hell, I don't know, that's the thing. She got sick in New York or something, was what we heard. Maybe she just thought better of it. Anyway, she didn't make it down here. My men waited for the next flight, almost two hours. When she wasn't on that one either, they gave up and went home."

It was beginning to feel like that's what I'd better do, too.

"Anything else?" Don was saying.

"One thing, quickly. An outfit on Chartres called the Black Hand. Check it out for me?"

"Don't have to. Part Panther, part populist politics. There's money from somewhere, and pull. Into everything. Run by a guy named Will Sansom, now calls himself Abdullah Abded. Lew, you're not mixed up with them, are you?"

"Curious, is all. Met a couple of their people."

"Well. That it, then?"

"That's it."

"Don't forget you owe me dinner and a drink. If I can ever get out of this bear pit long enough."

"I hadn't forgotten, Don. Give me a call. And hey, thanks."

Night had just about taken over, and lights were coming on block by block, the city's dark mask falling into place. In the next few hours those streets would change utterly.

Big money, Don had said. Hand in everything. Not my league at all. Just what the hell had I got myself into?

Chapter Seven

Now two weeks had passed and I had some idea what I'd got myself into, but I wasn't any closer to finding Corene Davis. And maybe I was as close as I was going to get.

I got up and dumped the rest of the coffee, lit a cigarette.

I had a feeling she'd made it to New Orleans. A hunch. I'd played them before and won at least as often as I'd lost.

I'd made the rounds with my clipped picture. No one had seen her. I'd been visited twice by Blackie and *Au Lait*. They hadn't seen her either.

What the hell, maybe she *was* sick in New York. Maybe she *was* kidnapped. Or maybe she was dead in a warehouse somewhere.

About all I'd really accomplished was to learn something about Corene Davis. It's strange how little is left of our lives once they're rendered down, once they've started becoming history. A handful of facts, movements, conflicts; that's all the observer sees. An uninhabited shell.

She was born in Chicago in 1936. Her father picked up what work he could, not much, all of it hard and hardly paid, her mother was a midwife, later a practical nurse. She'd gone to the University of Chicago on scholarship, become something of a student protest leader, then moved on to Columbia for graduate work, where she'd continued her protest activities while simultaneously becoming active (rare then for grad students) in student government. She had been investigated about that time, she claimed, by the FBI and, she suspected, CIA. Stood watching them tap her phone from a pole at the end of the block and took them iced tea when they climbed back down. But it wasn't until publication of a revised version of her master's thesis as *Chained to Ruin* that she'd become a full-fledged black leader. And so she'd made the round of talk shows and lecture circuits, been written about (as though the writers had encountered utterly different women) in everything from *Ebony* to *The New Republic*, and generally become a voice for her, our, people. A second book, on women's rights, was in the works. She had light skin ("She could almost pass for white," as one reporter put it), wore her hair clipped short, stood five-six, weighed in at one-ten, neither smoked nor drank, was vegetarian.

And had the capacity, it seemed, to vanish into thin air.

I stubbed out the cigarette in a potted plant LaVerne had given me and looked at my watch. Three ten. Maybe things would look better in the morning. It happened sometimes.

I drew a hot bath and had just settled in with a glass of gin when the phone rang.

"How you feelin', Griffin?" a voice said.

"Man, it's kind of late for games. You know?"

"You feelin' pretty good, huh?"

"Until some asshole called me."

The voice was silent. A dull crackling sound in the wires, witches burning far, far away. Then after a time the voice said, "You're looking for Corene Davis."

"Who is this?"

"*Don't*." And the line was dead.

To this day, I don't know who it was on the phone that night. But I remember the sound of that voice exactly, and the chill that came over me then, and I remember that I finished off the glass of gin and poured another before getting back into the tub.

Chapter Eight

COULD PASS FOR white.

I woke up at ten with that phrase rolling around in my head. I'd had a dream in which people were chasing me with knives down narrow, overhung streets. A big Irish cop watched it all, telling old minstrel-show jokes. The sheets around me were soaked with sweat.

I stripped and showered, then made coffee, real this time, and sat down at the kitchenette table, chrome and red formica. I lit a cigarette. Could pass for white. But her skin looked dark in the picture.

There's an old novel called *Black No More*, about a scientist who invents a cream that's able to turn black people white and the social havoc this brings about, written in the thirties by George Schuyler, a newspaperman. When I was a kid, Dad always used to grin when any of his friends mentioned it. And Mom said she'd whip me if she ever caught me reading it. Till I did, I thought it was about sex.

I walked into the other room, taking the coffee with me, and dialed LaVerne's home number. Not much chance, but worth a try. When there was no answer, I dialed one of the other numbers she'd given me and asked for her. I knew it was a bar she frequented most afternoons, picking up marks as they floated from posh uptown hotels down into the Quarter and back up. The guy that answered said, "Hold a minute, bud, I'll check."

I'd finished the coffee by the time she picked up the phone and purred into it, "Yeah, honey?" *Honey* had a few more syllables than it usually does.

"Lew. Listen"

"How's your father?"

"Holding his own, Mom says. It was a heart attack."

"You goin' up there, Lew?"

"Maybe later. Listen, need to ask you something."

"If I know it."

"This Nadie Nola cream: it work?"

"The girls say it does. Light, bright, and damn near white . . ."

I felt a warmth at the base of my spine, a tingling as though nerves beneath my skin were opening like tiny umbrellas, and knew it was all starting to come together.

"Thanks, Verne. I'll be talking to you. You get on back to work."

"I *am* working, Lew. You oughta see him over there watching me now, wondering who it is I'm talking to. Shoulders out to here and a wad of bills even Sweet Betty couldn't get her mouth around. Owns a funeral home up in Mississippi, he says. Must be good money in death up in Mississippi."

"Everywhere."

I hung up with something gone hard and cold inside me, thinking of Angie, a good enough kid till skag, Harry and her own deep sadness found her. Now her kid was living with her parents up near Jackson. She must be two or three by now, I guessed. And myself—what had I turned into? I could feel that wild hatred building up inside me.

There's this guy that lives uptown, Richard. Straight as straight can be, but every weekend he goes out and picks up rich white guys in hotel bars and the like, for sex, they think, and when he gets them alone, he kicks their faces in. I wondered if I was any better. My wife hadn't thought so.

I poured another cup of coffee and drank it, then unplugged the pot and headed for the car.

A photographer I know down off Lee Circle works cheap, doesn't ask or answer too many questions, and never minds a rush or difficult job if the money's right. I pulled the Cad into a spot in front of his place and got out. He was just getting there himself, standing at the door with keys in his hand.

"'Lo, Lew. Been a while, my man."

"Milt. Got a quickie for you, if you can do it."

"Come on in." He finished unlocking the door and waved me in ahead of him. "I can do anything. The wizard of the flash, they call me in polite circles."

"Oh yeah? When's the last time you saw a polite circle?"

"Skip it. What you got?"

"A picture I clipped out of a magazine. I want you to take it, lighten the skin, change the hair. It's a black girl.

When you get through with her, I want her to look white. Can do, wizard?"

"Let's see it." He took it and held it up to the light. "Well, at least it's on gloss. How much of a hurry you in?"

"An hour?"

"An hour, he says. All right. You wanna wait or come back?"

"I'll come back."

I pulled the Caddy out of its spot and headed for the Morning Call. Drank three cups of chicory and ate three beignets. A man across from me was reading the *Times-Picayune*, and I saw the headline on an inside page as he folded it back: CORENE DAVIS—WHERE IS SHE? So it was finally breaking.

I was back at Milt's on the hour. He handed me an eight by ten.

"It's grainy but the best I could do," he said.

I looked at the picture. Bingo. Barbie's sister.

"Can you put it on the tab, Milt?"

"Tab's kind of heavy, Lew."

I peeled off a fifty and shoved it at him.

"That cover it?"

"And part of the tab, too."

"Thanks, Milt."

"Anytime."

I got back in the car and sat there thinking. Now at least I knew who, or what, I was looking for. I even had a picture, a good one. Should I give what I had to Blackie, excuse me, Abdullah Abded, and let him take it from there? He had contacts and resources I didn't and might find her faster. Or should I go to the police—meet Walsh somewhere and let him play the thing out? I thought back to the newspaper headline buried on an inside page, business as usual, like no one really cared. Which is pretty much the truth of it, I guess.

Chapter Nine

So I hit the streets.

Parked at the Pigeonhole and walked across, car scooped up on a massive, lumbering forklift and served into one of the cubbyholes like a piece of pie behind me. Bourbon Street, first. If she'd never been in New Orleans before, there was a good chance she made the tour.

Louie at Pat's. Barney at The Famous Doors. Jimmy at Three Sisters. Daley at Tujagues. The best I got was a "Well, maybe." I even hit Preservation Hall and the Gaslight Theatre. But didn't hit paydirt till I'd worked my way down to The Seven Seas.

"Yeah, sure thing, she's been in here every other night this last week or so."

"Alone?"

"Not for long, but she always started off that way." Then, answering my sharp glance: "She was hooking. Had a look about her, you know? Fresh pony. Guys go for that."

"You're sure it's the same woman?"

"Sure? Sure I'm sure. The hair's different, but that's her

all right. Calls herself Blanche. Pretty heavy behind something, too, I'd say—out of a needle or out of a bottle. Hard to tell."

I wondered then: what was it that started a person sinking? Was that long fall in him (or her) from the start, in us all perhaps; or something he put there himself, creating it over time and unwittingly just as he created his face, his life, the stories he lived by, the ones that let him go *on* living. It seemed as though I should know. I'd been there more than once and would probably be there again.

Sooner than I thought, perhaps.

"Any idea where else she might be working?"

"Might try Joe's."

"She hasn't been there."

"Well. Place called Blue Door, then. It's—"

"I know where it is. Thanks."

"*De nada*. But how about a drink before you split?"

I ordered a double bourbon, put it down in one minute flat, left a ten on the bar.

So Corene had turned herself, or been turned, into a white hustler, I thought, driving out of the Quarter against heavy day's-end traffic and uptown toward the Blue Door. Stranger things have happened. Daily.

The guy behind the bar was Eddie, an ex-con. As a favor to Walsh I'd been a witness at the trial that put him away the second time. Once more and he was down for the count.

"Howdy, Mr. Griffin," he said when I walked in.

"Behaving yourself, Eddie?"

"Straight as an arrow, ask anyone. Sunday school, prayer

meetings. Right as rain." He looked toward the big window. "Speaking of which," he said, "raining yet?"

A few drops spattered against the glass and clouds rolled. "Not yet."

"Only thing about New Orleans. Rains every damn day." He went down the bar to wait on a customer who had just come in. Then he came back. "Something I can do for you, Mr. Griffin?"

"I'm looking for a girl, Eddie."

"Aren't we all."

"Calls herself Blanche. A hustler. You seen her in here?"

"Blanche. Hmmm, let me see now. 'Bout five-six, real looker?"

I nodded.

"That'd be Long John's girl. Brought her marks here a couple of times. Been on the street a week, two at the most. Fresh pony, you know?"

So now I was looking for two people.

"What's this Long John look like?"

"Mean mother. Real dark-alley material. Six-three or -four, maybe two-forty. Always wears a yellow suit. Never synthetics, always cotton. Says cotton is the American Negro's heritage. Heavy user."

"And where could I find him, if I looked?"

"Café du Monde or Joe's, likely."

"Thanks, Eddie. Keep your nose clean."

"Just cleaned it, didn't I? Cool as silk."

I went out wondering what Eddie had under the bar for *special* customers.

Chapter Ten

NOT WANTING TO go two out of three falls with the traffic, I grabbed a cab back downtown and had the driver drop me off on Canal.

A crowd was gathering on the sidewalk in front of Werlein's, doubled by its reflection in storefront glass among black pianos and shiny brass horns. I walked over, hearing about me a flurry of commentary, query, invective.

"Never knew what was coming."

"I seen it, seen it all."

"Bad blood 'tween 'em, had to be."

"Just like that, and it's over."

"Anybody call the police yet?"

One man—both were black—lay on the sidewalk in a mirrorlike pool of blood and urine. There was a sucking wound in his chest where the bullet had smashed its way in; each time he tried to breathe, the fabric around it, though blood-logged, fluttered. Then light went out from behind his eyes and his shirt grew still. He was done with all this.

Another man of about the same age stood over him with the gun hanging limply at his side, saying over and over to himself what sounded like "I done tried to tell him, I done tried to tell him." As though (I thought, walking on toward the Quarter), speechless and dumb for years, he had found at last a way to speak, to say the things he wanted.

Years later, as I stood in Beaucoup Books reading a poem in one of the magazines I skimmed from time to time there, that scene, something I'd never again thought of in all those years, came back to me full force. Once again I could see the shirt fabric flapping, the reflection of the crowd in the windows, the peace in both those men's eyes. *You must learn to put your distress signals in code,* the poem read.

Chapter Eleven

By the time I'd walked back into the Quarter, rain was imminent. I hurried down Chartres and through Jackson Square, with the smell of the brewery everywhere, to the Café du Monde.

He was sitting outside, in one of his yellow suits, with at least half a dozen empty coffee cups on the table in front of him. His pupils were as big as saucers. I could feel hatred building inside me, swelling, like the rain.

"Long John," I said. "Long gone, like a turkey through the corn—if I remember my blues. Lew Griffin. Where's Blanche?"

He looked at me out of those huge eyes.

"Now," I said.

"What, you got a thing for white, man?" he said.

"Just Blanche. Used to know her."

He seemed to be looking at something very far away, very private.

"She done changed since then," he finally said. He picked up one of the cups and peered into it as though he knew coffee was still there, as though its absence were only illusion: interesting, inarguable, but (nevertheless) soon over. "Let me turn you a nice nigger girl. Got some lookers in the bag, whatever you want, they be waiting. Young stuff. Foxes. Lady wrestlers."

I shook my head.

"It's Blanche or nothing."

"Then it's nothing," he said after a minute. He laughed and, raising his voice as if to order, said, "Nothing for *all* my friends. Lot of that going 'round, you know. Everywhere you look: nothing."

"All right. You probably know my name, Johnny, back in there somewhere, wherever you are. And that pretty face of yours, pretty as any of your girls—remember? Think about makeovers, Johnny. About what you could look like tomorrow morning, *n'est-ce-pas?*"

He looked across the table at me much as he'd looked into the empty coffee cup.

"Yeah, I know the name, Griffin. I done heard 'bout you. But she don't work for me no more, that's fact."

"I don't give a shit who she works for. No more than I give a shit about your pretty face."

"Yeah." His head drooped. Suddenly he was tired. "Yeah. I hear you. Thing is, I don't *know* where she is. I just don't know." Something flickered in his dull eyes. "Maybe still at the hospital."

"What hospital? What happened?"

He stared off toward the river. Atop the levee an old man and a kid were playing godawful trumpet and tap dancing tolerably together. I picked up one of the cups and smashed it down on the table. I went on grinding the shards into the table, blood running from my hand and pooling at the table's metal rim by his arm. He lifted a sleeve clear.

"Preparing your facial," I said. "Won't be a minute."

"Okay, man, okay. I hear you."

He pulled a handful of napkins out of the dispenser and dropped them on top of the blood, pulled some more and handed those to me, still looking off toward the river.

"Saturday night we're together and she just went plain wild on me, man. Crazy—you know what I'm sayin'? I cain't have no crazy woman workin' for me. So I dropped her off at the emergency room and left her there. What else could I do? And I knew they'd know what to do for her there."

"Which hospital?" I said. "Which hospital was it?"

He thought. "Let me see. Baptist. Yeah, that's it, Baptist. Cause I stopped off at the K&B up the street for a bottle when I left."

"And this was Saturday night?"

"Saturday night. She just went crazy on me, man." He looked back at me. Picked up one of the cups and tipped it back as though drinking. Dabbed at his mouth with the back of a hand. "Now what kind of girl was it you said you wanted?"

I wanted to kill him. Kill someone. Instead, I got up and walked away. I found a pay phone down the street, dropped in a nickel and dialed Baptist Memorial, asking for Admissions.

"I'm trying to find my sister," I said when I got through. "She ran away from home—Mom's worried to death—and we don't even know what name she was using other than Blanche. I heard she might have been hurt Saturday night and brought there."

"Just a minute, sir, I'll check." She was gone two or three minutes. "Sir, our records show that a Blanche Davis was admitted Saturday night. Negro, late twenties, early thirties. Could that be your sister?"

"Almost certainly. Could you tell me what room she's in?"

"Just a moment." A shorter wait this time. "Sir, our records show that Miss Davis is no longer a patient at this hospital."

"Can you tell me where she is?"

"This is your sister, you said?"

"Yes."

"Well, then I suppose it's okay to tell you. Miss Davis was transferred from our own psychiatric wing to the state hospital in Mandeville on Monday."

Chapter Twelve

HALFWAY ACROSS LAKE Pontchartrain I almost turned around and went back. The rain came down in buckets. Suspended there on the Causeway, both shores out of sight, I wondered: did I really want to know? That twenty-six miles was the longest trip of my life.

I drove through the gates and followed the signs that said ADMISSIONS. Pulled up in front of a cinderblock building painted green, got out, went in. After stating my business, I was told that Dr. Ball would be with me shortly. The waiting room was full of what I assumed were patients. They probably assumed I was too. A psychiatrist I'd gone to once, back when I was trying everything to keep my marriage and life from falling apart, told me I needed to be here.

"Shortly" was an hour and spare change. Time moves a little slower over here, I guess.

When I was finally ushered into his office, Dr. Ball said, "Mr. Griffin, I'm sorry to have kept you waiting so long, but as you can see, we're very busy here." An upper-Mississippi accent, edge planed away by college and ambition. He settled back in his chair. "Now, what can I do for you?"

"You're holding a patient calling herself Blanche Davis," I said.

"I'd have to check to be certain of that."

"Would you, please?"

He picked up the phone and dialed three digits, spoke her name, listened.

"That is correct, Mr. Griffin," he said, cradling the phone. "She's in Ward E."

"I wonder if you could tell me what's wrong with her."

"You are a relative, I believe?"

"Her brother."

"Well, then. As for what's wrong, I only wish that we knew. We seldom do, really. I can tell you that she's been drinking heavily. There are fresh needle tracks inside her arms, behind her knees. But I'm afraid she's too locked up in herself to give us much useful information. Perhaps your being here will help." He picked up a pen and tapped it once, lightly, on the desk. "We fear, Mr. Griffin, that she may be schizophrenic."

"I see." I didn't.

"You would like to see her?" Dr. Ball said after a moment.

"Is that possible?"

"Absolutely. It might well do her some good. All of us. The last thing we want is for patients to lose sense of whatever family there is. I'll call for a truck to take you over to the ward."

I waited outside and the truck showed up in about ten minutes. It was an old paneled job, green like the building. The driver was a cheerful-looking young man with long hair. He may have thought I was a patient.

"Ward E?" he said when I climbed in.

"Ward E."

That was the extent of our conversation.

He wound about the grounds and at last pulled up in front of another green building with oversize windows and covered walkways running off in all directions.

"It," the driver said.

I got out and walked through the nearest door. Halls converged toward a room to my left where a number of people sat reading magazines or watching TV. I walked in and back toward what looked like the nurse's station— either that or a tollbooth. *Mrs. Smith RN* got up and stepped out of it.

"You must be Mr. Griffin," she said. "Dr. Ball called ahead that you were on your way. Let me take you to her."

We went through a door into a dormitory room with maybe twenty beds. Then through another door—each one was locked—into a long hallway with windowed doors on either side. Halfway down the hall, the nurse stopped and fit a key into the lock of one of the doors.

"This is it," she said. "Try not to be too shocked. It's extremely difficult, I know. It always is, the first time."

She opened the door.

On a bed inside the room a woman lay staring at the ceiling, her eyes wide with fear. Every few seconds she would scream out—a silent scream—and throw her body against the restraints. Her exposed fingers worked at the air nonstop, like the legs of an overturned insect.

I had found Corene Davis.

Chapter Thirteen

As I drove back across the Causeway my mind rolled like the clouds that were still sending down a boot-heavy rain. I felt years of hatred, fear and anger draining out of me, a kind of rain itself, and I knew that Corene, the sight of her there in that locked place, had done that for me. Now what could I do for her?

One thing I *wasn't* going to do was tell Blackie and *Au Lait* where to find her, or what had happened. Maybe search out her people in New York and talk to them, confidentially. Corene needed friends now, not disciples.

Fame, pressures, loss of private time and life—what had done it to her? Or was it just something in her from the start, coiled up in there, waiting? I guess no one knew. Maybe no one would ever know. I found myself trying to reconstruct what happened between New York and New Orleans, to make a story of it, the plan, the execution. Getting on the plane knowing what she was going to do, her future in a suitcase at her feet. It all seemed so voluntary. But was she really in control? Or driven?

Finally, I guess, it wasn't that much different from the way we all make up our lives by bits and pieces, a piece of a book here, a song title or lyric there, scraps of people we've known, clips from movies, imagining ourselves and living into that image, then going on to another and yet another, improvising our way from day to day through the years we call a life.

I gave it up and sat watching the wipers slap rain back from the windshield. Every couple of miles there were small stations where you could pull off and call for help. There wasn't much else but water and sky and rain.

I thought about Harry. I thought about Dad and about Janie, my wife for just over two years, and my son. For a moment, as lightning flashed and the storm rumbled in its far-off heart, I became Corene again, as I had in a momentary flash back there: play of light and dark on the ceiling, gone even the words that would let me say what I watched, what I felt, what I had lost. But unlike Corene I had only to imagine a new life, and lean into it.

At the office there were the usual messages from downstairs and the usual accumulation of mail. A yellow envelope stood out from the rest. I picked it up and ripped it open.

YOUR FATHER DIED TODAY AT FIVE AM STOP FUNERAL FRIDAY AT TEN STOP CALL ME STOP LOVE MOM

I sat there for a long time without moving, thinking

how it had been: the expectations and disappointments, the fights, recriminations, misunderstandings, all of it getting worse and worse as time went by. But there were good things to remember, too, and finally I got around to them. Dad and me working on my first car in the backyard, a battered old Ford coupe. Getting breakfast together and watching day break in the woods above the town where we hunted squirrel and rabbit and came across Civil War miniballs which always brought him to thoughtful silence. The night he pulled out his old trumpet and played the blues for me that first time, when I realized that somehow he'd had a life before me, one that didn't have anything to do with me—and that my own pain was somehow the world's.

I lit a cigarette. LaVerne had the money, I had the time. Just call Blackie and tell him I couldn't find Corene, that's all there was to it. I'd be a free man in more ways than one. Then call Mom.

I finished the cigarette and reached for the phone.

Outside, the rain had stopped. The night was black like me.

Part Two 1970

Chapter One

NEW ORLEANS WAS sweltering. It hadn't rained in two weeks, and the temperature hovered around one-ten. Kids were turning on fireplugs—I guess they learned that watching the evening news—and older parts of the city didn't have enough water to flush toilets. There was also a garbage strike, and every fly that called itself American had moved south.

I was sitting in my new air-conditioned office downtown, reading *Pinktoes,* a book published by Olympia Press a few years back. I'd found it tucked in among girlie magazines at the all-night newsstand just off Canal at the top of Royal. It made me think back to the two years I'd put in at LSUNO, and it made me think, especially, of *Black No More.*

Not that the air conditioner was doing me any good, mind you. The city was having brownouts, and the mayor said we'd all have to cut back, be responsible. Yassuh. But I had to wonder where the mayor's thermostat was set.

I'd been back in town two days from a trip to Arkansas.

Mom was doing pretty good—of course, she'd had some time now to get over it, make the adjustment. She was probably as adjusted as she was going to get. My sister Francy had moved in with her and they seemed to be getting along all right for a change. Mom had put on a few pounds, Francy was dating a CPA. Things were looking up all over.

So there I was, ready for business, mail taken care of while I was away by a secretary I'd hired part-time from the secretarial college down the block. I had five or six thousand banked away, a reliable checking account, a charge card or two, and a new VW that was just about paid off. I'd been up to see the kid a month or so back. All I needed now was some work.

I turned on the radio, which told me it was ninety-eight degrees. I turned it off. That kind of news I didn't need. Sweat was already dripping down my shirt collar and pooling in the small of my back. And that was before I knew how hot it was.

I looked at my watch. Ten fifteen. It sure as hell wasn't going to get any cooler.

I picked up yesterday's *Times-Picayune* and glanced through it. All the headlines were about the heat wave, or the brownouts, or the president's trip to wherever, but right in along there, a little lower, were the usual burglaries, rapes and murders that make the world go round. Fine city, New Orleans. I'd been other places. It was still my favorite. Just don't ask me why.

I was back in the book; submerged in it like an alligator,

snout and eyes barely above water, half-living this story of
Harlem hostess Mamie Mason, Negro race leader Wallace
Wright ("one sixty-fourth Negro blood"), black journalist
Moe Miller who at last has to abandon both "the Negro
problem" and home when a rat (who's had the habit of
moving around the traps he sets so that he himself breaks
his toes in them) takes it over, and black novelist Julius
Mason, Mamie's young in-law:

> "Who's he?" Lou asked.
> "He's a writer too."
> "My God, another one. Who's going to be left to
> chop the cotton and sing 'Old Man River'?"
> Art chuckled. "You and me."

—both speakers here white. I made a mental note to
look up another book by the same writer mentioned on the
back, one titled *The Primitive*.

I had heard, I realized, or *thought* I had heard, a knock
at the door.

I waited but nothing else happened.

Finally I got up, walked over with the book in my hand,
pulled the door open.

A man and his wife—there was no doubt about that—
stood there. They were black and tired (a tautology?). He
wore an ill-fitting black suit, she a plain black dress. Probably their best clothes, and some pretty sad-looking threads.

"Can I help you?" I said.

"We hope so," the woman said. "We're," she said.

She looked at her husband. I guess it was his turn.

"We're trying to find our daughter," he said.

"I see. She's run away, has she?"

They nodded together.

"Have you folks been to the police?"

The man looked at his wife, back at me.

"They told us there weren't nothing much they could do. Said they'd check the hospitals and such. Said for us to keep in touch. We filled out this report."

"But they also told us," she said.

"They told us how many runaways there are," he finished. "They said for us to go on back home, she'd turn up, most likely."

"Back home. You're from out of town?"

He nodded. It looked like that was about all he could manage. "Clarksdale," he said.

"Mississippi," she said.

Where Bessie Smith bought it.

"And what makes you think your daughter came to New Orleans?"

"Just she was always talking about it, coming down in the summer when she could."

"Then you're probably right. How long's she been gone?"

"Three weeks now. Three weeks day before yesterday."

"A person can put a lot of distance between home and herself in three weeks," I said.

"But we're just," she said.

"We're sure she's here, Mr. Griffin."

"I was thinking of other things."

Together, they looked down at the floor.

"We know, Mr. Griffin. We know what can happen once they're gone. I seen it happen to my sister back home in McComb."

"But she's just sixteen," the woman said. "Surely she couldn't of got herself in trouble too bad, could she? We're Baptists, Mr. Griffin," she went on. "Not real good Baptists, but Baptists. We've been praying every meeting night, praying she won't forget or be led from how she was brought up."

I had a feeling the man had seen a lot more of life than his wife had. It wasn't just the way they talked; it was something set into the lines of his face. Strange how one person can live in the middle of a minefield, stepping over bodies, and never see what's going on around him, while another walks to the corner store for bread and in a hundred recondite images, shadows slouching in a doorway, light creeping up an abandoned building, sees everything.

"I hope," I said. "She have any money?"

He shook his head. "A few dollars. We ain't rich people, I guess you can tell."

We all stood for a moment looking at various walls.

"Can you find her for us, Mr. Griffin?" the man finally said. "We ain't got—we don't have much, but we'll pay what you ask."

"We pay our bills," the woman said.

"I'm sure," I said. "Well, suppose for a start you tell me your names."

"Sorry," the man said. "We ain't—we aren't quite our-selves. Clayson, Thomas Clayson. My daughter's name is Cordelia. This is Martha."

"Tell me a little about what your daughter's like, Mr. Clayson."

"Quiet, kind of shy. A good girl. Never had a lot of friends like some others. Always read a lot, ever since I can remember. Loved the movies."

"She was our pride and joy, Mr. Griffin," the woman said.

I thought: when the quiet ones finally break loose . . . I shook my head to clear it. The woman was still talking.

"—so hoped she'd go on to college, make something of herself. Saved all our lives for it. Skimped and saved and did without. And now—" She stopped. He looked at her as though he were going to say something, but didn't.

"What does she look like?" I asked.

"Well," he said. "She's a pretty girl. About, I don't know, five-four or so. They grow up fast, you know."

"Wears her hair short, with bangs in front," his wife added.

"I suppose you might have a picture?"

He reached into his wallet and handed me a snapshot.

She *was* pretty, with wide, alert eyes and thin, serious lips. In the picture she wore jeans and a light pink sweater. She looked a lot like a girl I'd known back home.

"How did, does, she usually dress? Something like this?" They both nodded.

"And you say she's been in New Orleans before. Any

idea where she might have liked to hang out, or any places she was especially fond of?"

This time they both shook their heads.

"Like I said, she don't—doesn't talk a lot," Clayson said.

"Any friends in the city that you know about?"

"She talked some about a girl named Willona. An actress, if that's any help."

"What kind of actress?"

"Actress, is all we know."

"You don't know where she lives?"

He shook his head.

"Look," I said, "I'll give it my best shot, but I just can't hold out a lot of false hope for you. This is a big, dirty city. It's way too easy to disappear into it—just like those bayous and swamps not too far away. And it doesn't much care about any of us individually, let alone a sixteen-year-old girl from Clarksdale. Where are you folks staying in town?"

"With my brother's family on Jackson Avenue," Clayson said. He gave me an address and I wrote it down. Over near the levee and New Orleans General, from the number. "There ain't no—isn't any—phone," he said.

"Okay then, I'll be in touch. There are a few things I can check out for you. Maybe something'll come of it. I'll let you know."

They turned and started for the door. They looked even more tired now, and I wondered for a minute if they'd make it through to the other end of all this, and how.

I looked at the snapshot again and said a prayer myself—for Mr. and Mrs. Clayson.

Chapter Two

THE CLOCK ON the bank at Carrollton and Freret said it was 102 degrees. I looked over at the palm trees lining the trolley tracks on the neutral ground opposite. The palms looked right at home.

I drove out to Milt's to have some copies of the snapshot made, then took Claiborne back down-town.

Don wasn't at his desk. A clerk went off to find him, and ten minutes later he came gliding in, shirtsleeves rolled up and sweat stains the size of mud flaps under his arms. His clip-on tie was lying on the desk like a museum relic.

"Hear about Eddie Gonzalez?" he said, sitting. "Went down for the count. Pushing coke at The Green Door."

He leaned back in his chair and let out a long breath.

"You've got three minutes," he said.

"I'll take two of them and keep the other for later. I've got a picture. I want it circulated to your men."

I caught the glint of suspicion in his eye. "Anything I should know about?"

"Just some kid whose parents want to find her is all."

"Missing persons is down the hall to the left, Lew."

"A favor, Don."

"Been a lot of those lately."

"I hear you."

"Okay, okay, you've got it. That all?"

I handed the copies over. "That's all. Thanks, Don."

"Right." And he was out the door.

I knew how it was. I'd tried it myself for a while, putting in time as an MP. Then the army and I came to an understanding: they would keep me out of a court martial and psychiatric hospital if I would quit busting heads and go on home. At the time it sounded like the best deal anybody ever made me.

I slid out of downtown headquarters and hit the streets. First the crash pads in the Quarter that pulled them in from all over the world it seemed, then those uptown. Actress, I kept thinking. All I knew about New Orleans theater was *Nobody Likes a Smartass,* which from every indication had been running continuously (and ubiquitously) from about the time Bienville founded the city.

Finally, at three or so in the afternoon, I walked into Jackson Square armed with a Central Grocery sandwich.

I hadn't been there for a long time, but nothing much had changed. A group of bluegrass musicians played by the fountain. Stretched out on the grass nearby were a number of hippies or freaks or whatever they were calling themselves those days—anyhow, they had long hair and their own aggressive dress code. I watched some of the girls in cutoffs and halters and suddenly felt old. Old and tired. Christ, I thought, just turned thirty and they look like kids to me.

I made rounds with my picture, then dropped onto a bench by one particularly fetching specimen of late childhood and ate my sandwich.

I waited.

After an hour or so I gave it up—lots of distractions and a nagging notion that the world might not be so bad after all, but no Cordelia—and wandered over toward the cathedral. I don't know why. Anyhow, halfway inside the door, about where they start selling trinkets to tourists, I turned around and walked back out.

Until 1850 or so, Jackson Square had been Place d'Armes, and it was there, during the years of Spanish rule a century earlier, that rebellious French leaders had been executed. A few blocks landward, in Congo Square, slaves were allowed to pursue music and mores otherwise proscribed by the Code Noir and *femme de couleur libre* Marie Laveau held court over regular Sunday voodoo rituals. Scenes from our rich heritage hereabouts. Laveau, incidentally, was said to have consorted with alligators. Obviously one hell of a woman.

That night LaVerne and I had dinner at Commander's Palace. Trout Almandine because they make the best in the city and a Mouton-Rothschild because we felt like it. The wine steward seemed a bit huffy at first but, as the evening went on, grew ever friendlier in proportion to the growing redness of his face.

"You know an actress named Willona?" I asked Verne at one point.

"Can't say I do, Lew. But lots of girls call themselves actresses."

We went back to the wine and small talk.

About two in the morning Verne's phone rang and she rolled over to get it. I could hear a heavy, almost growling voice on the other end, but couldn't make out words.

"Yeah, honey?" Verne said. More growling. "Really? Kinda late for a working girl, you gotta give better notice ... Yeah, sure, honey, I understand, of course I do ... Yeah, I know where it is ... I'll be there, sure ... Give me thirty, thirty-five minutes, huh?"

She hung up.

"Gotta split, Lew," she said. "One of my regulars."

I nodded and she swung out of bed toward the closet. She had more clothes in there than they had at Maison Blanche.

I waited until she'd left, then got up, dressed, and went home.

Chapter Three

HOME THESE DAYS was a four-room apartment on St. Charles where trolleys clanked by late at night and you could always smell the river. It had a couple of overstuffed couches, some Italian chairs, a king-size bed, even pictures on the wall. Mostly Impressionist.

I parked the bug on the street and went in. Poured a brandy and sat on one of the couches sipping at it.

I was thinking about Cordelia Clayson and the ways it could go. Maybe she was hustling on the street corners by now, I didn't know. Maybe she was into drugs, or booze. Or plain old for-the-hell-of-it sex. Or Jesus. Anything was possible. Whatever, I didn't feel too hopeful about the news that sooner or later I was going to have to bring her parents. I'd seen too many times what the city could do.

Actress, I kept thinking. Actress. I didn't know anything about acting, but I'd had a professor at college who had done a bibliography of New Orleans theater since 1868 or some such date, and tomorrow I'd give him a call.

Right now it was time for bed. I finished off the brandy, undressed, set the alarm for seven, and hit the sack.

I was wakened at six by the phone.

"Yeah?" I managed to get out.

"Lew? I'm calling from downtown."

"Don. Don't you ever go home?"

"Funny, my wife's always asking me the same thing. Can you come down here, Lew? It's Vice. They think they've got your girl."

I drove over expecting to talk to Cordelia Clayson in a detention room. Instead, I was ushered into a room on the fourth floor lined with books and what looked like cans of film. Don introduced me to Sergeants Polanski and Verrick and left. "Can't watch this shit, Lew. Daughters of my own," he said.

"Something we picked up at a party down on Esplanade," Polanski told me. "Thought you'd be interested."

While he was talking he threaded film into a projector. When he raised his hand, Verrick hit the lights and there we were, in dreamland.

A big white dude in black socks was doing things to a young black girl. Alternately fucking and sucking and beating and lecturing her on the philosophy of the bedroom and woman's natural submission. It sounded like something out of de Sade by way of Heffner and Masters and Johnson—the redeeming social significance, I guess.

It was cheaply made, frames jumpy, figures and faces out of focus. But the girl was undeniably Cordelia.

The film lasted maybe fifteen minutes. Nobody said a word the whole time.

"Your girl?" Polanski said when it was over and the lights were back on.

I nodded.

"Who made it—you know?" I said after a moment.

"Guy by the name of Sanders. You get to know them by their style after a while—camera angles, things like that. Bud Sanders. Rents a cheap motel room, turns a girl up high on speed or whatever's going, and rolls the camera. Mostly the men are the same ones over and over."

"You pick him up?"

"What the hell for?" Polanski said. "He'd be back out on the street before we started the paper-work."

"What about community standards?"

"You're kidding. In New Orleans?"

"We could try," Verrick added, "keep him busy a while. But it wouldn't be long. Nothing would stick. Water off a duck's back. Then he'd just go out and rent a new camera and start all over again."

I nodded. I'd seen porn films in my time, some in the line of business, a few for pleasure, but this one had really got to me. I was thinking about Mr. and Mrs. Clayson up on Jackson Avenue and what I'd tell them.

"Where can I find this Sanders?" I said.

"Who knows?" Polanski said.

"Turn over the nearest rock," Verrick said.

"What happens to the film now?"

"We hold it for evidence, then we file it. But there are probably ten, twelve copies of it on the streets by now."

"We can't keep on top of it," Verrick said. "You close one factory down, two more spring up. Like those dragon's teeth or whatever they were."

I nodded again. "Thanks, Polanski," I said. "Verrick— let me know how it turns out. What becomes of the girl? If you find her."

"Man, the girl's nothing. They pop out of the wood-work like sweat on a hog. It's Sanders we want. For good. The girl's yours, if we ever get to her. But we won't."

I started out the door.

"And you got a room full of this stuff," I said.

"This is just pending cases. You oughta see the vaults down at Central Holding," Polanski said.

It was only then, walking out the door, that I realized that I had an erection. It made me remember some of the things my wife had called me.

Chapter Four

THE ALARM CLOCK was still buzzing when I got back to the apartment. I poured a cup of coffee—it was on a timer—and filled a pipe. Then I reached for the phone.

I got through to Dr. Ropollo at his office in the English building and after telling him what I'd been doing the past ten years (it wasn't much, after all), asked him about Sanders.

"Bill Collins is the guy you need to talk to. Teaches cinema up at Tulane. But he's probably home, or in his studio, this time of day." He gave me the two numbers and I wrote them down in my notebook. I thanked him and hung up.

I poured another cup of coffee and tried the first number. Nothing. I dialed the second, studio number. It rang five times.

"Collins." A high, slightly effeminate voice, though businesslike at the same time.

I told him who I was and asked about Sanders.

"Bud Sanders, you mean? *That* asshole. Talk about birthright and a mess of pottage," he said. "Talk about pissing it all away. Be one *hell* of a filmmaker if he wanted to. *Horrible* waste of talent." He said it as though he were a man who couldn't tolerate much waste of any kind.

"You know where I might find him?"

"Well, he teaches a cinematography course down at the free school. You might get in touch with him there."

"Thank you, Mr. Collins," I said. "I'll let you get back to your epic now."

"Epic, hell. I'm shooting another fucking TV commercial for 'feminine hygiene products' is what I'm doing."

"I'll look for it."

"Along with the rest of the world." And he broke the connection.

The free school wasn't listed in the book and Directory Assistance had never heard of it. I finally called a flaky friend of mine, a stewardess who spent her off-time collecting lost causes, and got the address.

It was one crumbling building on the edge of Elysian Fields near I-10. From the look of it, it had been a hotel at one time or another. Now it was filled with long-haired sweaty kids and covered with graffiti. Don't drop toothpicks in the toilet or the crabs will pole-vault to freedom, it said on one wall. God is watching you, it said above that. I wondered if he (or she) was watching Cordelia Clayson too.

I finally tracked down the Administrative Offices on the second floor and walked in. A girl who couldn't have been more than fourteen got up from a desk and walked toward me.

"Yessir," she said.

"Yes'm. I'm looking for Bud Sanders, have a job for him but can't seem to connect. Wondered if you might be able to help me."

"A job, you say?"

"Right."

"Well." She considered. "You could leave a message with me, I'd see he got it."

"I appreciate that, but I'm afraid I'm in a hurry. I really have to get through to him today. If I'm going to use him, that is."

"Well." She looked around the room as though he might be hiding in it somewhere. "Wow, I don't know." She reached around behind her and grabbed her braids, tugged at them. "There's money in it for him, huh?"

"Yes'm. Quite a bit, really."

"Okay. Well, I don't think he'd want me to let you get away." That decided, she let the braids go. "He's on location. Belright Hotel, on Perdido near Tulane and Jeff Davis."

"Thanks, Miss."

"Ms."

"Right."

"Room 408."

Chapter Five

THE LAST TIME I'd been to the Belright was on my honeymoon. We'd ordered chicken sandwiches "with extra chips" and they'd brought enough for a party. They'd also sent up champagne and a fruit basket. I guess we were pretty happy there for a little while. But it was the beginning, still, of a long decline.

The Belright back then had been pricey and plush. Declines were everywhere.

I pretended I belonged there, walked through the lobby and up the stairs, something I wouldn't have gotten away with just a few years before. But now there wasn't a porter or other service person in sight, only one youngish, half-bald guy behind the desk picking his nose with a ballpoint pen.

I heaved myself up the four flights and knocked on 408, waited, knocked again. Finally someone opened the door an inch or so and stuck his nose in the crack.

"Yeah."

"You Bud Sanders?"

"Don't know him."

"Maybe I could introduce you."

Inside the room someone, a man, said, "Who's that?"

"Some wiseass nigger."

"I interrupt something between you two fellows?" I said.

He opened the door wider and glared at me.

"Look, fellow," he said. "We're trying to get a little work done in here. Why don't you just go away and let us get back to it."

"Now let's see. What kind of work would that be, in a hotel room with all those bright lights I see behind you there? PR film for the Belright, maybe? Hope your demographics are right."

"Goddamn."

It was the other guy. A second later the door opened and he stood there by Sanders, sweaty and naked at half-mast. I kicked him in the kneecap, then the stomach, and went on in.

The woman on the bed wasn't Cordelia. She wasn't conscious, either.

I spun around and grabbed Sanders by the neck.

"Okay," I said, "I had to see who you had in here. Now you listen to me. First, you get some help for this woman. Then you find Cordelia Clayson—shut up and listen—and you bring her to me at the fountain in Jackson Square by five o'clock tonight." The other guy was starting to get up so I kicked him again. "Don't make it so I have to come find you again. Be there."

"Man, I don't know where that girl is."

"Find out." I let go of him. "We're through talking. You better wrap it up, he's not gonna feel much like fucking anymore."

I went out, down the stairs, through the lobby. Going back outside felt like walking into a forest fire. Sweat burst out of every pore I had.

There were piles of garbage in plastic bags in the alley alongside the hotel. You could hear flies buzzing inside them, their sound amplified by the taut, membranelike plastic.

Chapter Six

WALSH AND I finally got together for lunch that afternoon at Felix's. He was standing at the bar just inside the door when I got there, staring at an oyster.

"Somehow I always expect them to scream right before they go in. You know, suddenly grow a little mouth in there, and cute little round eyes, like in Disney cartoons."

He shrugged and downed it, his last, and we grabbed a table being vacated by two fortyish guys wearing tiny old earrings, shorts and not much else.

Both of us ordered po'boys and beer.

At some point during the meal, and for no particular reason, I asked Don about his father. He shrugged.

"Didn't really know him much. Left, or my mother threw him out, or he got put away, whatever, when I was, I don't know, nine or ten, maybe. What I do remember's not good. Lots of hollering and being stood in corners or sent to bed, a few beatings—more, toward the end. Usual happy American childhood, right?"

"Close, anyway. Seems like it."

I bit off a plug of hard bread, shredded lettuce, hot sauce, oysters. Chewed.

"Mine never touched me. Never said much, but you could see the world going on back there behind his eyes. Had this kind of private smile, mostly. I didn't know *him* very well, either, not even what he did for a living. He'd go away for long periods, months sometimes. And he'd always be a little . . . I don't know . . . different, when he came back. Nothing you could pin down, but different. Like whatever he'd been away doing had changed him. And so I had all these different fathers coming home every time. But I didn't know any of them, not really."

A drunk stumbled up on the street outside and pressed his face close to the glass. The black man in livery shucking oysters behind the bar gently shooed him away.

"I remember one time I was nine maybe. I'd done something pretty terrible—stolen dimes from a jar of them my mother kept in the closet, I guess. They were standing in the doorway to the room where both of us kids slept, and they must have thought I was asleep. 'You've got to lay hands on him this time, George,' she was telling him. And after a while my father just said, very quietly, 'I will not bring violence into my home, Louise. I've lived by it too long.' The next few times he left, he stayed away longer, then one of those times he didn't come back at all. After a while Momma moved us in with relatives."

"Jesus, Lew."

"—has nothing to do with it, as Mae West said." I finished up my beer and signaled for two more. "Anyhow, I made all that up. Nothing mysterious or dangerous about him. He was just an ordinary man."

Don looked at me a long time. "Sometimes I think you just may be as crazy as everyone says you are."

"I am. Sometimes."

We drank our beers.

"Ordinary," Don said. "I used to be that, I guess."

"Well, good buddy, whatever else happens, at least you're still white."

"Yeah, there's that." And putting down the empty glass: "You want to get some air?"

We walked down Decatur to the French Market and trudged over the levee. A cool breeze eased in off the water. Due south along the river's curve lay the city's bulky torso, flanked by the wharf with its growth of ships, tugs, barges. The Canal Street ferry was just pulling out of its slip heading at an angle toward Algiers.

That camel's hump of land over there, directly opposite oldest New Orleans and now the city's fifth ward, is central to its history. At various times called Point Antoine, Point Marigny and Slaughter House Point, in the last days of French rule it was the site both of the colony's abattoir and powder magazine—and a depot for shipment after shipment of slaves newly arrived from Africa.

Dr. King had a dream. I at least had History.

Chapter Seven

I spent the rest of the day making phone calls and wondering. Maybe I should have stayed there at the Belright and called Vice. They wanted Sanders; maybe something in the scenario—whatever it turned out to be—would have led us to Cordelia. But Sanders himself seemed, as they said over at Jefferson Downs, a better horse.

Still, I didn't really expect him to meet me. I figured it might take two or three times to convince him I was serious. And next time he wouldn't be so easy to find.

I was half right.

Just as I was leaving the office to head for Jackson Square, the phone rang.

"Griffin? Sanders, Bud Sanders. I asked some people about you, man."

I let it hang there.

"They said you're crazy as shit. Someone told me you killed a man you didn't even know up near Baton Rouge a couple of years back."

"The girl, Sanders."

"Look, give me some time—a day, right? I'll do what I can."

"Noon tomorrow, call me then or before. And Sanders?"

"Yeah?"

"Don't disappear."

"Disappear, hell. I'm getting easier to spot all the time. Got cops sitting out in the alley waiting to go through my goddam garbage, my wife's lawyers on me like fleas. Now I gotta have you burning my ass."

"Reaping what you sow, Sanders."

"And what about you, man? You ain't no goddamn pope yourself, now, are you?"

"Noon. Tomorrow."

I hung up.

And what *about* me? Back when I found Corene Davis I'd thought my anger, my hatred, was gone forever. I'd been on top for a long time now, even chipped off a little corner of the good life for myself. But it was a lie, a story that didn't work, a piece of white man's life, not mine; and now the anger and hatred were coming back. I had kicked that guy in the hotel room in the stomach. I had wanted to kill him, kill them both. Robert Johnson's hellhound was nipping at my heels.

I tried a couple of numbers for LaVerne and didn't get her, so I figured she was with a client. Not much wanting to be alone just then, not *really* alone, but not with anyone either, I drove over to Joe's.

Happy hour was in full bloom. One guy had already

zonked out, face down on one of the corner tables, but everybody kept buying rounds for him and lining them up in front of him. There were the usual jokes about Joe's hard-boiled eggs. Two guys were throwing darts in the back, with a *Playboy* picture of Ursula Andress tacked to the board. Nipples were automatic wins.

Nancy asked me what it was going to be and I said it was going to be scotch. To see her, you'd think Joe was violating child-labor laws. She looked fifteen and was twenty-four, with three bad marriages already behind her and another (I'd met the guy, and there was no way) looming on the horizon.

She brought the scotch for me and an orange juice for herself. I've never known her to drink.

"How ya been, Lew? It's been a while."

"*Ça va bien,* as our friends from the swamps say."

"Yeah, I took French in high school. Had this teacher, one of the best-looking guys I've ever seen. He'd sit on the edge of the desk, throw his hair back, it was real long for them days, and he'd recite these poems and things. And I'd be looking at his pants the whole time, cause he wore them real tight, and you could see his dick laying there on his left leg. Looked absolutely huge." She took a swig of o.j. "Found out later he was queer."

"*C'est la vie.*"

"How's Verne?"

"Fine, last I saw of her."

"She working?"

"Guess so."

She finished off the o.j. and rinsed her glass, put it mouth-down on a towel.

"I get off at eleven, Lew."

I didn't say anything.

"Yeah, well, like you say: *C'est la vie*. Such as it is. You want another, you let me know. That one'll be on the house."

"Joe doesn't believe in the concept of 'on the house,' as near as I can recall."

"What Joe don't believe in is coming in once in a while to find out what the fuck is going on." She laughed. "Got him a new young honey."

"At his age?"

"Ain't no age limit on love, Lew."

"How about 'at his size,' then?"

"There's always ways."

"Right. Wills and ways. What does Martha have to say about this?"

She shrugged. "What's Martha said about all the others? She'd better be clean, not in his house ever, watch the money, knock on my door when it's over."

After a few more scotches I joined the dart throwers and hit four nipples in a row. Goaded on by them, I ate four of Joe's eggs, then we started in together on the drinks lined up by the zonked guy at the corner table. A long time later I realized that Nancy had her purse and was standing by the door.

"Hey, you coming with?" she said. "Or not?"

"With," I said. I was wobbly on the way to the car,

hers, but I rolled the window down and let air blow in my face all the way to her place and got at least halfway straight.

In her bed, one mattress stacked on top of another, we held one another closely, and soon slept.

Chapter Eight

I woke up feeling like the inside of someone's shoe.

There was a clock on the floor beside the bed and it read 9:43. In the kitchen there was coffee and soft music and a note that said "Thanks, Lew." There was also, warming in the oven, breakfast.

A cross and a heart-shaped locket hung together from a magnetic hook on the refrigerator.

I finished off the pot of coffee. I couldn't face food but dumped it in the toilet and flushed, so she wouldn't know. I showered off the whiskey's sour smell, her perfume, a little bit of my shakiness and shame.

By eleven I was at the office. There were three messages on the machine. One was from Nancy and said I wish there could be no past, only the present and a future. The second was from Francy, to tell me that Mom was sick with what they were calling an acute depression. The last was from Sanders. Come out to Algiers, he said, 408 Socrates.

I was heading out the door when the phone rang.

"Lew?" LaVerne said when I answered. "Back off Bud Sanders. Please."

I didn't say anything for a while, then I said, "I don't know where this is starting, I don't know what's being said here."

"You don't have to. Shit, you have to *understand* everything?" I heard ice cubes clinking against a glass. "He's a good man, Lew. Everything's coming down on him now and I don't know how much more he's gonna be able to take."

"You're telling me he's a client."

"No." Ice again. "I'm telling you he's a friend, Lew. For a long time now."

"Like me."

"Right."

"And you know what he does for a living?"

"Just like I know what *I* do for a living. What you do for a living. What we all do, one way or another." She took another drink. "We aren't angels, Lew. Angels couldn't breathe the air down here. They'd die."

"Right. But I need some information, Verne."

"He'll give it to you. But Lew—"

"Yes?"

"I think he's in love. I don't know if he can let her go. Be gentle with him, try to understand."

"For you?"

"Whatever." Ice clinked again against glass. "I'm drunk, Lew. I can't afford to be drunk; this is one of my regular spots."

"I'll come and get you, Verne."

"No, I'll be all right. Just switch to coffee and sit here a while. You go on. But Lew?"

"Yes?"

She was silent for several seconds.

"Everything's so shitty, Lew, so fucked up. It doesn't have to be like this."

"I don't know," I told her. "I've been trying to figure that one out for a long time."

"No one ever has. Ever will."

"You sure you're gonna be okay?"

"Yeah. Yeah, I'll be fine. You be careful. You're not real good at being careful, Lew."

"I try."

"Don't we all. Bye, Lew."

"Bye, girl."

I started out again, then came back and sat at the desk, staring out the window. I felt as though I'd lost something, lost it forever, and I didn't even know what it was, had no name for it. Those are the worst losses we ever sustain.

Chapter Nine

NEW ORLEANS NATIVES accent the first syllable and allow the entire word only two: So-crates. God knows what we'd do with Asclepius. Socrates is part of an old section of houses chopped up into apartments and strange corridors that would be slums in any other city but here are just where poor folk live. A lot of them, oddly, seem to be black. And of course they're only poor (so the rest of the great American fairy tale goes) because somehow they choose to be.

I took the wrong turn off the toll road and ended up over in Gretna in a warren of Hancock, Madison, Jefferson and Franklin streets. Why not, here of all places, one named for Sally Hemmings, Jefferson's slave-mistress?

I drove back across into Algiers, past driveways filled with junked cars, oil drums and abandoned refrigerators, past storefront churches, bail bondsmen, a martial arts academy, an Ethiopian restaurant, a boarded-up florist, ten blocks of project housing, an overgrown park, and a Bible college, and found Socrates.

Four-o-eight was at the edge, where things had started back up the ladder, a typically grand old New Orleans home renovated within the last ten years and divided (judging from nameplates by the front door) into three apartments. One of the plates read *W. Percy, M.D.*, another *R. Queneau.* The third one just read *B.S.* I punched the button beside it. I punched it again. Nothing.

The front door, however, was not locked and led into a foyer with twelve-foot ceiling and stained-glass skylight. Two of the apartments were to the left of an ornate curved stairway leading, presumably, to an upper hallway or balcony, if to anything at all. The third apartment was to the stairway's right, and that door was unlocked too. I went in.

A narrow hall ran to a well-equipped kitchen at one end, an unoccupied living room, strangely jumbled with antiques and chrome-and-glass, at the other. A ladderlike stairway climbed through the ceiling in one corner and took me into a bedroom smelling of young women— powders, perfume, polish remover, Noxzema. Some clothes were tossed onto the floor by the bed. A Bible was on the bedside table. There was a connecting bathroom, then another bedroom.

I went to the bed first. She was alive but not spectacularly so, deeply drugged, no reaction to a hard pinch, blood slow to come back. Once I figured she was going to be okay, I turned to him in the chair, but there wasn't anything I could do for him.

Most of what had been his head was splattered against the wall. His hand had fallen into his lap and remained there, the gun, a forty-five, on the floor between his feet. I smelled urine, feces, the animal scent of blood and tissue.

By the wall across from him a camera sat on its tripod, still filming. I didn't touch it. But I went back down the stairway to the phone in the living room and dialed downtown.

"Walsh," I said.

"Sergeant's with the Chief. Can I—"

"Get him."

"I couldn't inter—"

"Get him, *now*, or he'll have you for breakfast tomorrow."

A pause. "Could I say who wants him?"

"Lew Griffin."

I waited all of a minute.

"Lew, what the hell?"

"Four-o-eight Socrates," I said. "Our friend Sanders has just checked out permanently."

"Twenty minutes," Don said. "Don't wander off."

Chapter Ten

A CRUDELY LETTERED title card drew back from the screen and there was Sanders, holding it in one hand, pointing to it like a mime, face contorted into a gigantic smile. It read: *Last Film*.

He turned his back to the camera and walked slowly to the chair. When he turned around and sat, his expression had changed to a tragic one as exaggerated as the earlier smile. He mimed wiping tears from one eye, then the other. For a moment he hung his head, then shook it sadly again and again.

But an idea was starting up in his mind, and as it formed, the smile slowly returned, more natural now, less exaggerated. He held out his hand and, magically, a forty-five appeared in it. Waving good-bye with one hand, with the other he put the barrel of the gun into the smile.

And that was how I had found him.

"Jesus," Don said.

Polanski and Verrick looked at one another, shaking their heads.

"He and the girl were living together?" Don said.

I nodded.

"How'd you know that?"

"Someone told me," I said.

"*Who* told you?"

"I forget."

"He the one that drugged her?"

I shrugged.

Don looked back up at the blank screen.

"This is one fucked-up world. And the best we can do is shovel shit from one place to somewhere else for a while."

"You need me for anything else, Don?"

"No. Go on, Lew. Be careful."

I walked down the four flights of stairs and outside. An old man in rags was sitting on the sidewalk with his back against the building. "Lock me up, officer," he told me.

It was a little after nine and had probably been dark thirty minutes or so. A haze of heat and light shimmered over the city. Breathing was like walking in wet tennis shoes.

I retrieved my car from the police lot where Don had checked it in, and drove out Poydras to Hotel Dieu.

At the nurse's station in intensive care I explained who I was and was told that one of the doctors would see me shortly, please wait in the family room outside. The fear, pain and blinding hope in that room were palpable. At length a tall, stooped young man in yellow scrubs came to the door and said quietly: "Mr. Griffith?"

"Griffin," I said.

"About Cordelia Clayson?"

"Yes, sir."

"Please come with me."

We went back into intensive care and to a small room at the far end. He pulled the door closed. Through it I could hear the sound of alarms going off, a voice saying: I need some help over here.

"And just what is your relationship to the patient, Mr. Griffin?"

"As I told the nurse, I'm a private detective engaged by the girl's parents."

"To investigate what brought her here to us?"

I shook my head. "To find her for them. My job's done, except that now I have to go and tell them. And I need to know *what* to tell them."

"I see. You're in touch with the parents, then."

"I know where to find them."

He had sad brown eyes. You wondered if they would stay that way, or if after years of this (he couldn't be more than twenty-six or -seven) they would harden.

"I can't hold out a lot of hope," he said. "It's not the drugs themselves, of course; we've learned how to handle all that. But Cordelia had a hard hit of some unusually pure heroin. She was out for a long time, and what happened was, she developed what we call shock-lung syndrome. The heart slows down dramatically and loses the force of its contractions, so that everything kind of backs up. Her lungs are full of fluid. They're hard to inflate—every breath is like the first time you blow into a balloon—and oxygen levels in the blood are critically low. We're doing what we can. She's on a ventilator that does all her breathing for her, and she's receiving hundred-percent oxygen at high pressures. But we're not gaining much ground, Mr. Griffin. And frankly, the interventive measures we've been forced to use are more likely to lead to further complications than to any resolution of the original problems. We get in this sort of downward spiral after a while. I'm sorry."

I stood. "Thank you, Doctor. Will Mr. and Mrs. Clayson be able to see their daughter if I bring them down here? Are there restricted visiting hours?"

"Not in this case, Mr. Griffin. I'll leave instructions at the desk."

I went out through the double doors to the elevator. In the family room, every face turned toward me.

Chapter Eleven

THE BREEZE HAD turned into a steady, low wind and there was rain in the air. I drove slowly along Melpomene thinking about parents and children, how so many homes were war zones these days, how love breaks under the weight of years and words and disillusion, how as we get older, more and more, we see our parents' faces in the mirror.

I swung onto St. Charles and up into the Garden District. There are entire streets here where you go burrowing down tunnels of green, trees curving over and around you, sky shut away. It reminds you how much of New Orleans is pure artifice—that it's a constructed city, dredged out of swampland by sheer force of will and labor, nibbled at constantly by history, the river, the swamp's dark mouth. For most of the 1830s the New Basin Canal, meant to assure American self-sufficiency from Creoles, was hacked out with pick and shovel (there was no dynamite, and no way to keep swamp seepage out except back-breaking pumps from Archimedes' time) at a cost of well over a million dollars and at least eight thousand lives. A hundred years later the city of New Orleans voted to refill this canal.

It was as though the city's image of itself, and the ways it tried to live up to that image, kept changing. It was Spanish, French, Italian, West Indian, African, Colonial American; it was primarily the city of fun and illusion, or primarily the bastion of culture in a new land; it was a city built on the backs of slaves and simultaneously a city many of whose important citizens were *gens de couleur libre;* endlessly, it adapted.

I parked on Jackson Avenue and found the address I wanted behind one of a row of apartment houses: what used to be a slave's quarters connected to what used to be a garage by a room narrow as a sidewalk.

"I'm looking for the Claysons," I said to the man who opened the door.

"You'd be Mr. Griffin?"

"Yes."

"Please come in." He backed out of the doorway.

Mr. and Mrs. Clayson were sitting inside on a shabby love seat and stood to introduce me to Clayson's brother and his brother's friend. I knew the friend from the streets, a working girl whose specialty was impotent men and rough trade with other women. I wondered if this was home for her.

As gently as I could, I told them about Cordelia and asked if they'd come with me. Mrs. Clayson closed her eyes and said under her breath what I suppose must have been a prayer. Mr. Clayson looked off at the wall as though he'd just lost whatever faith he'd had up to this point. They stood, and we walked out into the beginning rain.

By the time we reached Hotel Dieu, it was pouring. I let the Claysons out by the front lobby, told them to wait for me there, and parked. Six steps from the car, I was soaked through.

We went up in the elevator. I left them in the family room and stepped through the double doors. The doctor I'd spoken to earlier glanced up from a stack of charts at the nurses' station, then walked toward me shaking his head.

"She's gone, Mr. Griffin. Just a few minutes ago. It was her heart, finally. It couldn't take the strain any longer, I guess, and she arrested." He held his fist out, slowly opened it. "You'll want me to talk to the girl's parents?"

"I'll tell them, Doctor—unless they ask things I don't know. You'll be here?"

"I'll be here."

"Thank you."

"I didn't do very much, Mr. Griffin."

I went back through the double doors, took the Claysons out into the hall and said what I had to say, then stood waiting through their silence.

"I'll take you folks home whenever you're ready," I finally said.

Mrs. Clayson looked at her husband, who was staring out the window into the rain. We could hear the storm breaking around us.

"I reckon we're ready now, Mr. Griffin," she said.

I was getting into one elevator behind them when the other opened.

"You folks go ahead. I'll be right down," I said.

LaVerne had just stepped off the other elevator. We waited until they were gone.

"She's dead, isn't she, Lew?"

I nodded. "You know the rest?"

"I know." She looked at the same window Clayson had been looking out. "You think he knew he was killing her? God, he loved her so much—like he was a kid himself, you know?"

"I don't know, Verne. I don't think he did."

"You ever love anybody like that, Lew?"

"No."

"Think you ever will?"

I shook my head.

"Me neither."

"I better be going, Verne. Her parents are waiting."

"Lew." She looked back from the window. "Will you come stay with me tonight? I don't want to have to think about myself tonight. I don't want to think about—" She moved her mouth but no further words came.

"I'll be there."

She just nodded. Something in her face made me think of when we'd first met, how beautiful I'd thought she was and all I had felt for her that night so suddenly, how I would have done anything then to make her feel safe and happy and cared for—anything. Though I couldn't tell any longer how much of what was left was feeling, how much only memory.

Chapter Twelve

I DROPPED OFF the Claysons, who were slowly turning to stone, and told them again that I was sorry.

"We'll be expecting a bill, Mr. Griffin," Mrs. Clayson said, handing over a scrap of paper with their home address penciled on it.

They wouldn't be getting one, though. I drove uptown with my thoughts in tow. The rain had run most drivers off the streets; only good ones, and the fools, remained. One of the latter had just tried sliding into home under a trolley. He didn't make it.

I was remembering all the women I'd loved or thought I would. Thinking how that felt at first, how the feelings declined, how they stayed around for a while like locust husks on a tree and then one day just weren't there anymore.

LaVerne met me at the door in what could not possibly have been the gown she was wearing when we first met but looked just like it. She said nothing. On the coffee table inside sat chilled scotch, a pitcher of martinis, a plate of cheese and fruit, mixed nuts in a round silver bowl.

I pointed to the pitcher and she poured martini into a glass of ice. She poured herself one as well, without ice, and we sat there, two lonely people together for however long it would last.

I thought of lines by Auden: "Children afraid of the night/Who have never been happy or good."

Verne leaned against me and shut her eyes.

"Why do things always have to change, Lew? When I was a kid my mother'd have a new man around the house every few months—wasn't that often, but seemed like it, you know how it is when you're a kid—and I kept wondering why she couldn't just find one she liked and leave those others alone. Never occurred to me that she didn't have much to say about it. That the world wouldn't be the way she wanted it, the way any of us want it, just because we want it so bad."

She sipped at her drink and we sat there quietly for a while, each with his own thoughts.

"I used to ride trains a lot. Mama'd put us on one and give the conductor fifty cents to look out after us. And I'd sit in the end car and watch everything pass by, all those places and people I'd never get to know, gone for good—and so quickly."

She looked up at me.

"I'm still on that train, Lew, I've always been. Watching people I've loved go away from me, for good."

She looked into my eyes for a long time and then made an odd, choked sound. I don't know if she had tried to make a train sound or if it was a sob, but I reached for her there on the couch as, outside, the storm began to quieten.

Part Three 1984

Chapter One

LIGHT: IT SLAMMED into my eyes like fists.

I groaned and tried to move my arms. Someone had put sandbags on them to hold them down. I was incredibly thirsty. The air reeked of alcohol, vitamin capsules and fresh urine. Red hair floated above me somewhere.

"I wou'n't be trying to move about too much, sir," a voice said, each *r* a tiny engine turning over, almost catching.

"Where am I?" I asked.

"You're in Touro Infirmary, sir." Again, those *r*'s. "The police brought you here. Welcome back. Try to rest."

Everything kind of floated away then, and for a long time there were just snapshots. Some kid about nineteen who said he was a doctor, holding the garden hose he said he was going to "run" down my nose. He didn't. Dozens of lab people with Mason jars they needed to fill with blood. A guy in a three-piece suit who sat as far away from me as he could get and wanted to know how I was handling all this.

Gradually days fell into place. Lab work before breakfast, a perfunctory visit from your doctor about ten, group at eleven, lunch, kitchen duty, thirty-year-old travel films, TV, evening medications, lights out at ten.

After three or four weeks I said, "There was a woman."

"Lots of them."

"She took care of me in the beginning, when I was really in bad shape. Scottish, I think."

"That'd be Vicky. She's over at Hotel Dieu, I hear." This one was short, Latin, hair in a thick braid. "I never did understand why those British nurses are all so damned good. But if *I* was sick, that's who I'd want taking care of me, bet money on it. You need anything else, Mr. Griffin?"

"No. But thanks, Donna."

"Por nada."

This went on for some time. I remember my father sitting beside the bed for a week or two. Verne came in a few times and told me if there was anything she could do . . . Corene Davis bent down and whispered something in my ear, which later Earl Long tried to bite off. One night Martin Luther King was there, but nobody else saw him. I asked.

"Lew?" someone said. "Lew? You okay?"

It was Don. He looked a lot older than I remembered him, a lot tireder. "You need anything, you better let me know." He told me his wife had finally left, taking the kids with her. He said one of his people had picked me up and they'd kept it quiet.

"What do you feel about all this?" he said.

"Jesus, Don, you sound like one of the shrinks around here. I feel fucking embarrassed, is how I feel. *Mortified*, as Daffy Duck used to say."

"You were pretty far gone, Lew. Ever since you and Janie got back together and it went bad again. I guess you know I was sending jobs your way."

"I knew."

"But finally I had to stop. I couldn't answer the questions those people came back to me with. You remember much of how it was the last few months, Lew?"

I shook my head.

"My men had standing orders. Every night they'd find you about twelve or so and see that you got home. You didn't *want* to go home, but you did. Sometimes they'd take you home three or four times a night."

He paused and I said, "That bad."

"One morning the captain wanted to see me. 'Who the fuck is this Lew Griffin', he said. 'He a dealer, a stooge, what?' I told him you were a friend. 'They don't pay us to take care of friends, Walsh', he said, they pay us to scrape the bad guys off the streets, keep a little order out there. I'm not telling you anything you don't already know. I said, 'Yessir.' He said, 'I'm not going to hear this name anymore now, am I?' I said, 'Nosir.' But my men still had that standing order."

I started to say thanks, but Don said, "Just shut the fuck up, Lew, all right?" I did. "Then a night or two later I get this call from Thibodeaux. I'd promised Maria we'd have that night together, it was our anniversary or some damn thing, and between the second drink and salad the beeper lets loose. It seems the waitress at Joe's had called. For about an hour you'd been methodically walking into one of the walls there, saying you were trying to find the bathroom. The guys picked you up, I came down and had a look, and I told them to bring you up here."

"My thanks."

"I didn't hear it." He looked closely at me. "You've given me some grief, Lew. More than I'd ever have taken from just about anyone else. One thing you never did, though, was bullshit me, ever."

"Right. But when, and how, do I get out of this rabbit hole?"

"You're court-committed, old friend. For what the laws call a reasonable period of observation."

"Which means that I'm delivered, without reservation or restraint, into the hands of those for whom I'm an ever-renewable meal ticket."

"Lew. Think about where you were, man."

"Have you met these guys, Don? I tried to shake hands with one of them and I thought he was going to leap over the couch and run out the door. My so-called social worker has an American flag pinned to his lapel. There's Muzak in every fucking corner of this goddamn place, even in the bathrooms. Yesterday I heard a synthesizer version of Bessie Smith's 'Empty Bed Blues.'"

"Things'll get better, Lew."

"Now *you're* bullshitting *me*. Things never get better, Don. At the very best, they only get different."

He stood there a moment, then said, "Seems like it, doesn't it? I'll do what I can, Lew. Money, a place to stay, someone to talk to. You let me know."

"I will."

He nodded and left.

That week they decided the detox was complete and took me off sedatives. I was feeling pretty shaky, and the dreams weren't near as interesting, but it wasn't too bad. The rest, they said (three of them talking about me among themselves behind stacks of folders while I sat cross-legged on a folding chair at the front of the room), could be handled on an outpatient basis. A couple of days after that, they let me go. Don had dropped off some clothes. I sat in new navy polo shirt and chinos staring across at a bug-eyed accountant until he stopped making noises about my bill and discharge payments and so on and said all right I could go.

It was cool outside, and overcast: gray. The world didn't look too much different from the way I remembered it before checking out for a while, only noisier, faster. But then, it wasn't the world that had changed. I felt like someone long underwater, sucking in those first lungfuls of precious air. And at the same time I felt weighed down out here, overcome by so much activity, chance and change.

I took a cab to the Napoleon House—Don had dropped off some money with the clothes—and ordered a double scotch. Sat there looking at it, and being looked at by the waiters, for two hours. Then I got up and left.

I really didn't know where to go. I'd given up paying

rent on the office a long time ago, and I was sure I didn't have an apartment anymore either. Sun goin' down, black night gonna catch me here. Finally I stopped at a phone booth, dropped in my nickel, and dialed Verne's number, the new one.

"'Lo," she answered.

"It's Lew, Verne." There was a pause.

"Can't get away from the past however fast we run, can we?" she said. "I'm sorry, I didn't mean that the way it probably sounds. How are you, Lew?"

"Better."

"I heard."

"Walsh?"

"My husband golfs with one of the docs who watch-dogged you at Touro. You gonna be okay, Lew?"

"I'm gonna try to be. But I'm going to need a place to stay."

"That's easy. Take the old place on Daneel; I kept it for sentiment's sake. Key's where it always was."

"Thanks, Verne. Be happy."

"Lew! Wait a minute. Some guy's called for you; I almost forgot. God only knows how he got this number. Hold on. I've got a note here somewhere . . . William Sansom. Ring any bells?"

"Never heard of him."

"He wants you to call him."

"He didn't say what about?"

"Nothing. But the number's 524-8592. Anytime, he told me."

"Right. Later, Verne."

I hung up, dug out another nickel and tried the number. A breathy female voice answered "Yes?"

"William Sansom, please."

"I'm afraid Mr. Sansom is out of the building just now. May I say who called?"

I told her.

"*Ou* or *ew?*" she said. "Excuse me, sir . . . Mr. Griffin, I'm sorry, but Mr. Samson *is* in after all. Will you hold a moment? Thank you, sir."

Stevie Wonder music came on the line. Moments later, a heavy male voice.

"Lew Griffin! How's it going, man? You okay?" He stopped, and I said nothing.

"You may not remember me, Mr. Griffin. We met some years ago, and you knew me then as Abdullah Abded."

"Of course," I said. "The Black Hand. Finger in every pot, just like the chicken in every."

"You got our check, I hope."

"You know I did."

"We appreciate what you did, Griffin. You keep up with what happened with Corene? She went back to school, got her M.D. Now she's in South America, traveling from village to village down there, doing what she can. There's no stopping the woman."

"So what'd you need?" I said.

"Not me: you. Heard there'd been some hard times for you, Griffin. Thought we might be able to help."

"Yeah?"

"Heard you were just out of stir and maybe needing a place to stay. We run a halfway house down below the Quarter—some junkies, a few ex-cons, a lot of lost souls. Low batteries needing some time off the rack. You'd be welcome."

"Why?"

"Anyone's welcome. But you're a brother—*and* you've helped us in the past."

"Got my own tracks, though."

"That's cool. But if it comes to it, don't forget us. This number is always good. Take care, man."

"Right."

I went up to Canal and walked around a while in the streams of shoppers, tourists, folks grabbing a half or whole hour off work, others hanging out aimlessly at bus stops and corners. Outside Maison Blanche, Sam the Preacher was holding forth on evil, atonement and the eternal struggle for rebirth. Sam's been at his post for over twenty years and never, as far as I know, missed a single day, rain or shine—or hurricane, for that matter. The last couple of years there's been a kid with him most days, maybe twelve or thirteen, who plays hymns on trumpet what little time Sam's not preaching. In a city famous for its eccentrics, and proud of them, I guess Sam and the Duck Lady are king and queen. Every so often she still shows up in the Quarter pulling a little wagon behind her, with a string of ducks of all sizes quacking along behind that.

I walked down toward the river and along the levee, smelling hops and yeast from the brewery, smelling stagnant water and things that grow in it.

It was, after all, a kind of rebirth. No home, no work or career, just a lot of loose connections: a whole life to build from scratch. The terms *tabula rasa* and *palimpsest* drifted into my mind from courses taken long ago at college. And what was it, that Irish guy who wrote in French, something like: I can't go on . . . I'll go on. It was getting colder, and a steady, low wind blew off the water. Barges crept upriver toward Memphis or St. Louis. A riverboat, dance band playing on the foredeck, was filling with afternoon tourists.

I thought about a test they'd given us back in school, when I was in the ninth grade maybe, around fifteen or so. Dozens of questions like this: "You have been at sea a very long time. The captain is a cruel, unjust man. One night some of the sailors come to you and ask if you will lead a mutiny. What would you do?" Results came back and our parents were called in for a conference. "Lewis made excellent decisions, fine choices," Mr. Pace, the adviser, told them, "but there's something missing from the profile. He doesn't push, doesn't *strive*." "We already knew that," my old man said, and got up and left.

Riverside, a guy and his kid were playing awful trumpet duets of "Bill Bailey" and "When the Saints." I wandered back toward the Square. In one corner a young white clarinetist and an old black tenor banjo player worked their way through popular forties music; in another, an old trumpeter and young guitarist, both white and looking vaguely European, were doing Dixieland with complicated harmonies.

I went across to the Café du Monde and had a couple of coffees and an order of beignets. Then I bought a piece of sugar cane at the Market and was walking back up Chartres toward Canal to catch the trolley, sucking at the sugar cane, when a Pinto pulled up beside me.

"Griffin? Spread 'em," the man said. I did, leaning forward onto the car. It gets to be habit after a while.

One of the guys flashed a badge, not local. The other one turned me around to face him.

"Okay, Griffin, you're clean. Where you living?" I shrugged.

"No known address," he said to the other one. "Got a job?"

I shook my head, thinking how ancient this encounter was.

"No income," he said.

"Been offered a place to stay, though," the one with the badge said.

"That right?"

Their conversation went on without me. "The halfway house."

"Well. Maybe you better take that offer, Griffin."

"Yeah. Be a real good idea."

"Then maybe you could kind of keep an eye on Sansom and his people for us. We know something's gotta be going on down there."

"We just don't know what."

They both got back into the Pinto.

"You need money, Lew?"

I shook my head.

"Sure you do. Everybody needs money. You be thinking

how *much* you need and let us know. We'll work something out. See you, Lew."

I watched the Pinto drive away down Chartres, hoping someone would rear-end it.

Chapter Two

"I AM PLEASED that you reconsidered," Sansom said. He wore a dark suit with suspenders and looked like a lawyer. "More coffee?"

I shook my head.

"We've put you in room C-6. Only a couple of other guys in there right now. Any problems, let me know. Usually we ask for some work in return, but you've already done yours. Come and go as you wish. Make any money, throw in the pot whatever you think's right. There's food laid out in the common room every day between four and six—cold cuts, fruit, cheese, soup, bread."

"I met some people on the way here," I said.

"Let me guess. Guys in gray suits with short hair and rep ties? Yeah, they think we ought to still be painting slogans on ghetto walls instead of actually *doing* something. I don't know, maybe they think we're stockpiling bombs in the basement. We don't *have* a basement, man— this is New Orl*eens*." For a moment intelligence fell away from his face and he became a caricature. "We don't be good niggahs, Massuh Griff 'n." Then he laughed, a deep, rolling laugh. "Come on. I'll take you up."

The room was surprisingly light and airy. Beds occupied each corner, a small round table and chairs took up the room's center. There wasn't much else: a squat bookcase, some shelves nailed to the wall, a couple of throw rugs.

"Where is everyone?"

"Jimmi—" He pointed to one of the beds, meticulously made. "—does volunteer work with a child care group and is out most days. Carlos—" This bed was unmade. "—passes out flyers, telephone books, whatever work he can get. You never know, with him. Bathroom's at the end of the hall to your right, towels and all that on shelves behind the door. Again, you let me know if there's anything else you need; otherwise, we'll all leave you alone." He stuck out a hand. "Glad you came, Lew."

I was kind of glad too. I lay on the bed watching the ceiling and wondering what the next move should be. When I woke up, it was dark outside.

I wandered downstairs to the common room. A couple of guys were hunched over a chess set, a half-dozen others were circled around a TV showing the last scenes of *The Big Sleep*. Dinner was long gone and I was starving.

I remembered passing a Royal Castle on the way there, and headed for it. Not many people on the streets—too damned cold—and not many people in the R.C. either. One guy with a beard and scraggly thin hair drooling onto his french fries; a young couple making out in the back booth; two Wealthy Independent Businessmen talking over the charts and invoices spread between their baskets of burgers. The clock said it was 9:14.

I had a mushroom burger, baked potato with sour cream, coffee. My first real food for a while, if you could call it that. It all smelled of bacon grease and tasted as though it had been cooked by the same person who invented polyester.

I paid the cashier, which put a hefty dent in my ready cash. She didn't punch out prices but merely hit keys carrying stylized pictures of a hamburger, a mushroom, a potato, a steaming coffee cup.

"Come see us again real soon," she said.

"Had a great time," I told her.

I meandered along Basin, gradually aware that a car was pacing me. Turned into a side street and the car followed, against the one-way sign. Finally just turned and waited for them.

"Spread 'em, Griffin," one of the guys said. I already had.

"You thought over what we were talking about earlier?" I shrugged.

"Man needs friends in today's world, especially a black man, right? You a friend of ours?"

I shrugged again.

"Man don't know if he's a friend of ours, Johnny."

The guy in the car shook his head sadly.

"Makes you wonder who he *is* a friend of. Hello: what's this? Johnny, you see this, don't you? Where'd it come from?"

"Came out of his inside coat pocket, Bill."

"And what is it?"

"Looks like a bag of some kind of white powder, near as I can tell."

"You writing all this down?"

"Check."

"You going out to do your laundry, Griffin? This some Tide or Cheer here?"

"Don't think so, Bill," the other one said.

"Nope. Ain't Tide or Cheer. What *is* it, Griffin?"

"You tell me."

"Looks like high quality coke to me, Mr. Griffin. I'm quite surprised you don't recognize it."

"Never saw it before."

"Sure, Lew. No one ever has. Amazing how no one ever sees any of this. Right, Johnny?"

"Right."

"You writing all this down?"

"Right."

I walked—mainly because of the lawyer who materialized from nowhere and told me, the desk sergeant and then the court that he represented a rehabilitation center operated by "one William Sansom and Associates." Somehow he managed to get a judge down there and had me in the courtroom for a prelim within the hour. The judge was a woman of fifty or so who listened closely to everything, yawned a couple of times and said, "No P.C. It's out." I saw Walsh standing at the back of the courtroom. He and the two feds exchanged glances as they left the courtroom.

It was nearly midnight when I got back to the place. The TV was still on, but nobody was there watching it. Upstairs one of the bunks held a snoring body cocooned in sheets. On another a guy sat nude, reading *Principles of Economy*.

"You must be Lew," he said. "Glad to have you with us."

I nodded, went down to the bathroom, came back and stretched out on my bed with a copy of *Soul on Ice* that I'd found by the john.

"You read a lot, huh?" he said after a while.

I lowered the book. "Couldn't afford much education, and couldn't sit still for most of what I *could* afford. I've been trying to make it up ever since."

"You read Himes?"

"Much as I could find in used-book stores."

"Hughes?"

"Every word."

"Don't run into many readers," he said. "I'm Jimmi. Jimmi Smith. Used to be a teacher. Loved it. But I couldn't leave the kids alone."

"Girls?"

"Boys. That bother you?"

"Not especially. *Chacun à son goût.*"

"I help take care of kids now at day care centers, but we only take girls, this outfit I'm with, so it's cool."

"That's good."

"Yeah . . . You got family, Lew?"

Sansom stuck his head in about then and said, "Good. You're back."

"Thanks to the lawyer you sent. How'd you know, anyway?"

"We know everything that happens around here, sometimes *before* it happens. But I have to tell you, our lawyer's out of town on some business for us."

"Then who . . . ?"

"A friend of yours."

"Walsh."

"I didn't say it. But it was obviously more . . . politic, to have the lawyer appear to be from us. Good night, guys."

"You were asking about family," I said after a while. "Yeah."

"Why?"

"I don't know," Jimmi said. "Never had much, I guess. Wonder what it's like . . . Got a sister."

"Only the two of you?"

"Yeah."

"Where's she?"

"I don't know exactly. About a month or so back, letters started getting returned. Tried calling her, the phone's disconnected. I just hope somehow she's okay."

"You two close?"

"Only person I was ever able to love. Only one who never held anything against me," Jimmi said.

We slept then, and in the morning he made no move to resume conversation. Carlos rose wordlessly from his bed, inhabited the bathroom for a quarter-hour, dressed and departed. I drank coffee in the common room and watched morning news on TV, trying to figure out what had gone down in recent months. How it all fit together, if indeed it did. If it could.

Those first weeks in hospital had been the worst, as I surfaced and sank, rolled back to the top and again subsided, skin barely able to contain me, insensible things at march just inside it. The only good thing about that time was remembering Vicky, how she helped me get through it all and that wonderful soft voice, and I wanted to thank her. At least that's what I thought. I probably wanted a lot more, even then; we usually do, don't we?

I could get nothing out of a suspicious personnel secretary at Hotel Dieu and finally went upstairs for more coffee at the cafeteria. I asked a few nurses there about her, but they were even more suspicious. Often being around other people is like coming face to face with a mirror: your blackness suddenly becomes indisputable fact.

I had a couple of cups of chicory, ordered some toast with the second, and sat watching all the faces. People losing loved ones or about to, watching them die by degrees; others trying to console with visits and small talk or scripture; some annoyed at the interruption to their lives of minor, but necessary, surgery or tests; those who took care of the interrupted and dying alike. And others who helped new lives, not so gently, into this very old, ungentle world.

By this time it was almost noon. I had paid at the counter and was just reaching to push my way out when I looked up and saw her through the glass door.

"Mister Griffin," she said. "How are you?"

I said I was fine and asked if she'd mind my joining her.

"Not at all. I'm always alone for lunch."

We settled into a corner booth. She ordered a salad and looked a lot younger than I remembered. I had more coffee. The waitress kept looking over her shoulder at us.

"I wanted to thank you," I said. "I don't think I'd have made it through all that without you."

"Of course you would have done. Our best character shows up when we're down, doesn't it? And I'm paid well enough, here in the States, that I don't need any thanks, really." She lowered her head. "But I am glad you came to see me."

Neither of us said more, until after a while, picking at her salad, she said, "I've been here fourteen months. I know a few of the people I work with, two people who live in the apartment complex close to me, and that's all. Every month I think: I ought to go back home."

"I'm glad you didn't."

"Maybe I am too, just now."

We sat there finishing our coffee and salad and looking at one another. Finally she said, "I must get back onto the floor now, Mr. Griffin—"

"Lew."

"Lew. But I hope that I'll be seeing you again."

"You will if you want to, Vicky."

We were standing outside the cafeteria, in the mall, by this time. Currents of people broke around us.

"I want to. I'm thirty-five, Mr. Griffin. I've had affairs with a few men, been engaged twice. But I really want to get married, maybe even have kids. Perhaps that scares you."

"Very little scares me after what I've been through."

"Good, then." She pulled a pad out of her pocket and scribbled quickly on it. "Here's my phone number and address. Call me."

"What's best for you? What shifts and all."

"Anytime. Mornings at seven-thirty are good; either I've slept the night through or am just coming in from work. Ten or so evenings, too. You're almost sure to catch me then. Mostly I work nights."

"Okay. Soon then, Vicky."

"I do hope so. *Au revoir.*"

New Orleans natives tend to swallow or drop their *r*'s; that's why, to outsiders, the prevailing white accent seems most unsoutherly, in fact distinctly Bronx-like. Vicky's *r* was in marvelous contrast. She caressed each one as though she loved it, as though it were the last she might be privileged to utter.

After she was gone I looked down at the paper in my hand. It was from a notepad advertising a "mood elevator" put out by one of the pharmaceutical companies. That seemed wholly appropriate.

Chapter Three

SOME LIGHT MUST shine behind our lives always, one of my college teachers said. He'd been a poet, apparently a good one, well thought of, promising. The light was draining out from behind his life the year I had him for freshman lit. Halfway through the second semester he didn't show up for class two days in a row. They found him on the floor of his bathroom. He'd hanged himself from a hook in the ceiling above the tub, and though the hook had torn out of the rotting plaster, his throat was already crushed and he had died after a few moments' thrashing about in fallen plaster, back broken across the edge of the tub in the fall.

Meeting Vicky, getting to know her, I felt the light start up again behind my own life. It hadn't been there for a long time.

I started doing collections for a loan outfit over on Poydras. Walsh had vetted me, and I was still big enough and mean-looking enough to be effective pulling in payments for them. They started me out on a token salary, soon added a percentage, then doubled the salary as well.

Vicky and I were seeing one another pretty regularly: concerts, dinner, films at the Prytania, theater, museums, long afternoons over espresso or bottles of wine. I recalled the concept of monads—whole areas of knowledge, of understanding, which opened entire to the developing individual. And felt new worlds opening within me, worlds I'd always known were there but couldn't find, couldn't get to.

This whole period, like those early weeks in the hospital, but for quite different reasons, is something of a blur to me. I tracked people down all day, clocked out at six or so and headed for Vicky's, and we either went out somewhere or stayed in talking and listening to music until she had to leave for work herself. My hours were flexible, and on days she was off I'd sometimes work at night to be with her during the day.

Work, a waiting woman, money in the bank, personal growth: American dreams.

But I stayed on at the halfway house. Carlos grudgingly began telling me *buenos dias*. Jimmi, the few times we were there simultaneously, didn't want to talk. Vicky asked me to move in with her. Sansom came by every Friday to be sure everything was all right.

Time passed, as it will.

Both Verne and Walsh called to see how things were going. *Ça va bien*, I told them.

The president began another covert war.

Memorials were erected to those who'd died in the *last* covert war.

The CIA overthrew small South American govern-
ments and kept thick files on many of its own citizens.

Business as usual in South Africa.

Russia growled at us and we growled back—nothing
new there.

Down by the Mississippi River Bridge they were
swarming like ants, building for the '84 World's Fair.

I moved in with Vicky.

It was a rather fashionable apartment complex, and
she'd made her small corner of it forever British by hanging
pictures from the cornices, setting two morris chairs beside
a low tea table and otherwise filling the flat with heavy, old
furniture. There had been the usual compact, synthetic
furnishings when she moved in, she said; she'd felt she was
living in a motel. There were books everywhere.

One night after we'd been together a few weeks and
had decided to stay in for the evening—I had a pot of red
beans simmering on the stove and was about to start the
rice—there was a knock at the door. It was Jimmi Smith.

"Bill Sansom says you're good at finding people," he
said without preamble.

"Your sister?"

He nodded.

"Please come in," I said, and introduced Vicky.

"I've got a bad feeling," he said. "Something's happened.
I can't go on like this anymore."

"Will you stay for dinner, Mr. Smith—please," Vicky
said.

He shook his head but a little later let himself be led to

the table. He was talking about how they used to sit on the swing in the backyard and spit grape seeds at each other, how they went everywhere together in their matched overalls. I poured wine and Vicky brought in fresh French bread. Over dinner and through a second bottle of wine he told me about his sister, Cherie. Gave me her last address and a small photo, an old school picture, the only one he had, he said, because she never liked having her picture taken.

"I'll poke around and see what I can come up with," I told him. "I'll be in touch. You're still at the house?"

"Same bunk, same book."

I showed him out and started stacking dishes. Vicky had picked up the photograph.

"She looks so very young."

"At our age, everybody starts looking young. Cops look like kids to me these days."

"She also looks like someone who knows the best part of her life is already over," Vicky said, and was sad the rest of the night. In the morning I checked in at the loan company, picked up my slips and, finding two of the leads out in Metairie, where Cherie's last address also was, headed that way.

The first lead took me to an apartment house reminiscent of rabbit warrens where a dirty-faced adolescent female opened the door along a length of chain and said, "Yeah?"

"Your folks home, young lady?"

"Naw. Ain't never home 'fore 'leven or twelve."

"You get your sweet little butt back over here, LuAnne, and tell whoever that asshole is you're busy," a voice said inside the apartment.

"You know where I might reach them at work?"

She shrugged.

"Excuse me, LuAnne," I said, and kicked the door in.

He was on the couch, thirty-eight or forty maybe, wearing a double-knit leisure suit with the pants pulled down around his ankles.

"Don't bother getting up," I said. "If you do, I'll kick your balls into Oklahoma. Go put your clothes on, honey," I told the girl. "You know about statutory rape, mister? Even prison-yard hardasses take a dim view of it."

"You a cop, man?"

"Are you out of here?"

"You told me not to move. 'Sides, I'm the girl's uncle."

He was coming up off the couch and I kicked him in the belly. He grunted and fell back.

"This is a *child*, asshole."

After a while, when he was able, he hauled himself afoot, pulled up his pants and left. The girl looked after him, tears forming in her round eyes.

"World's full of them," I said.

"I loved him," she said.

The second lead came up just as empty: a used book and record store not far off Veterans near Causeway. It had that fusty, peculiar smell they all have. A girl of twenty or so sat behind the counter braiding lustrous black hair that, unbraided, must have reached her knees.

"I'm looking for Frances Villon," I said.

"Frances Villon?" Tentatively.

"I was given this address. I could have the spelling wrong." I spelled it out. "She'd arranged a loan from us."

"Frances Villon." First with an English pronunciation, then the French. Her eyes wandered off and came back. "I get it—François Villon."

"What?"

"You've been had. François Villon was a fifteenth-century French poet. I don't think he'd be in need of any loans just now.

'I am François to my great dismay,
Born in Paris, up Pontoise way;
By a fathom of hempen cord I'll sway
While my neck discovers what my buttocks weigh.'

Someone's idea of a joke, huh?"

"Any idea who might be inclined to that kind of joke?"

"Not really, but it's kind of appropriate."

"What do you mean?"

"Villon himself was a professional thief."

The address I had for Cherie Smith led me to a converted garage apartment behind a lumberyard. It was empty; through the front window I saw only a sack of trash and some sweepings on the bare floor. I tried the door. It was locked.

Walking around back to look for a rear door or usable window, I discovered another, larger garage apartment. A tall, stooped young man with longish stringy hair was just backing out the door.

"Come to see the place?" he said.

"You the agent?"

"Showing it for them. I'm on my way to class, but I've got a few minutes, if you want to look it over. There wouldn't be any problem with your renting it. You know . . ."

I knew only too well.

"To tell the truth," I said, "I was looking for the former tenant."

"You a cop?"

"Do I look like a cop, son?"

"You sure as hell ain't her daddy."

"Friend of her brother's. He asked me to find her, if I can. Hasn't heard from her in a long time. He's been worried."

"Not much I can tell you. She stayed pretty much to herself. Never had people over, didn't go out much."

"She work?"

He shrugged. "I guess."

"When'd she leave?"

"Let's see . . . Close to a month, must be."

"You know why?"

"Couldn't make the rent. Owner finally had to ask her to move out."

"Did she?"

"The very next morning. Cleaned the apartment up and all before she went, too. Not many'll do that anymore."

"No forwarding address?"

"Not with me, not with the post office. I know because the owner was going to send back part of the deposit even though she missed the last month's rent. Felt kind of bad about the whole thing, I guess."

"Okay. Listen, I don't want to keep you, but if you happen to think of anything, anything that might help, could you give me a call?"

I handed him a card and a ten dollar bill.

"I can't take your money, Mr.—" He looked down at the card. "—Griffin?"

"Sure you can."

"Wouldn't feel right about it."

"All right. Then you just keep it a while and if nothing comes up, you send it back to me."

"Well," he said.

"Listen, I've held you up. Which school you go to?"

"Loyola."

"Then let me drop you. Wouldn't be a problem. You know . . ."

He grinned. "I *would* appreciate it, if you're sure it's not too much trouble."

"Not at all."

I dropped him off amidst armies of long legs and round bottoms in tight jeans and perfect breasts under sweaters, thinking I'd never make it to class in all that. Or wouldn't have—more years ago than I want to think about.

I headed back downtown, brewed a pot of coffee at the apartment—Vicky was on a rare day shift—and had just poured some Irish into it when the phone rang.

"Mr. Griffin?"

"Yes."

"Kirk Woodland."

I waited.

"At the apartment a little while ago."

"Oh. Right."

"I just thought of something, might help you. There's this kid down the street from where I live. He's, I don't know, eighteen or so, but really retarded, you know? Cherie used to go see him a lot, tell him stories and all, try to teach him things. You think she might show up there sometime?"

"She might indeed. Thank you, Kirk. You know the address?"

"No, but it's the only two-story wood house on the next block south. Can't miss it. White with yellow trim."

"There'll be twenty more coming to match what you have. I'll shove it under the door."

"No, Mr. Griffin. This is more than enough."

"I insist. You may have saved me a lot of time and work. And I never knew a student who couldn't use an extra dollar or two."

"Well," he said.

"Can I ask you something?"

"Sure."

"You have trouble concentrating with all those fine young ladies around all the time?"

"Doesn't everyone?"

"God, I hope so. I hope it's not just old men like me."

"Not hardly."

"Good. And thanks again."

I finished the Irish coffee, and another couple of cups without the Irish, and headed back to Metairie. LuAnne was still alone and without parents, Frances Villon remained a thief, and at the two-story wood house I met only suspicion.

I finally convinced the father (Mom had split a long time ago) that I wasn't a welfare officer or child molester (they probably came down to the same thing in his mind) and was introduced to Denny.

"She was real good with him, Cherie was. Only body ever spent any time with him save me."

Denny was not only eighteen, he was a giant, almost as tall as myself and built like a linebacker. He had full, slack lips and brown eyes that never blinked. He didn't talk, but made soft cooing sounds.

"When did you last see Cherie, Mr. Baker?"

"She came by, just for a few minutes, last week. Said she couldn't stay 'cause of a job interview but she had missed Denny so much."

"Say anything about when she might make it by again?"

"Said a couple of days. That was Tuesday. Guess she must of got tied up with the new job or something, huh?"

"If she does come back, Mr. Baker, could you give me a call?"

"You're a friend of her brother, you say?"

"Yes, sir. I can give you his number, if you'd like."

He looked at me for several moments. "I don't need his

number," he said. "When you live with someone like Denny, who can't ever tell you what's inside him, you learn things most people don't know. I see the pain and confusion in your face. It's been there a long time. But I also see you're a good man, and I know you're telling me the truth."

I nodded, and he told me he'd let me know when Cherie showed up again. "She will," he said. "It's just a matter of when."

Isn't everything, I thought, and headed back to town.

Vicky was home, sitting on the couch with a gin and tonic. She'd taken off her uniform pants but still wore the top, underpants, white stockings. Something about those white uniforms is sexy enough anyway, and it was accented by her pale skin and red hair.

"Posing for *Penthouse?*"

"For you," she said, raising her glass. "Want a drink?"

"I'll get it. You look tired."

"I've had a terrible day. A man we were ambulating died, just dropped dead right there in the hall with family and all the rest of the patients looking on. Then all afternoon it's the head nurse I have to put up with, going on and on about quotas and priorities as I'm trying to catch up on my work."

I got my drink, we both sipped, then she went on, her words as ever falling into natural cadences, so musical and lilting you could sink into the sensual pleasures of the language itself and lose meaning altogether.

"She refers to patients as 'units.' An acutely ill patient is twenty-five units, a bed bath is two units, an IV is one unit, and on and on. And on." She sipped again. "It's *rather* like a facto*r*y, isn't it?"

"And shouldn't be?"

"Can't be. Because things a*r*e changing all the time, patients' conditions, thei*r* needs. You can't ve*r*y well plot that out on pape*r* now, can you?"

"But the managers, that new, huge and ever-increasing class, must have *some*thing to do." I slipped into a dissembling voice, a mixture of Amos and Andy and sixties cant. "When duh rev'lushun cums, dose wif briefcases gone be de furst shot."

Vicky didn't feel like cooking, we both felt like eating, and the only thing in the fridge was very leftover lasagna. The choice came down to ordering from Yum Yum's, the Chinese restaurant a few blocks away that delivered, or going out somewhere. We had another drink and thought it over. Images of Yum Yum's greasy paper food cartons (like the kind used to carry goldfish home from the dime store) helped the decision immeasurably.

Chapter Four

We walked for a while and wound up at a Creole café run by an ageless Cajun and his family. Two kids about nine or ten were seating customers and clearing tables; a girl of thirteen or so was the waitress. The menu was chalked on a board by the door to the kitchen.

We each had a fish soup, fiery red beans and rice, *boudin*, all of it eased considerably by a chilled bottle of white wine. The bill came to $28.66—I swear I don't know how the man makes a living. Bouchard came out himself in his bloody, grease-smeared apron as we left, to make sure everything was satisfactory. We told him, as we always did, that it was *far* more than satisfactory, it was indeed and in fact excellent. "*Merci*," he said, and fled back as though relieved to his beloved kitchen.

We were walking aimlessly back toward the apartment, enjoying the flush from the wine and the chilly air, when a car slowed and pulled alongside us. There were two young white guys in it. One had a quart of beer, the other a fifth of whiskey, and they kept passing the bottles back and forth.

"Hey look," one of them said. "This nigger's got him a white girl. Must think he's cock of the walk now, huh?"

"Hey, man, you cock of the walk?"

"Talkin' to you, nigger."

I turned, looked at them, waited. This was an old, familiar scene, only the minute particulars of which ever changed. Nothing would happen until they got out of the car. And then it had better happen fast, before they were ready for it.

"Nigger can't talk," the driver said.

"Must be one of them *dumb* niggers."

"Bear shit in the woods?"

They laughed, drank, laughed some more. The one on the passenger side reached for the door handle.

"I've heard of things like this happening in the States," Vicky said, "but I di'n't believe it, not really. I guess every country must have bloody buggers like these two, though."

Everything was very still and quiet for a moment there.

"Shee-it, man," the passenger told the driver. "She ain't even a white woman, she's a damn foreigner."

They switched bottles once again and drove off.

"Welcome to the ghetto, Miss Herrington," I said, and we fell against one another laughing, laughing as one does only after great tension has passed.

Back home, Vicky drew a tub and came back through the living room naked to pour herself a brandy.

"You ever wear clothes?" I asked her. She made a face at me and licked her lips.

I put on some Chopin, low, and checked the answering

machine. This is Vicky, I'm out just now, please leave your name, etc., then the same thing in French. Sansom and Walsh had both called to see how things were going. Jimmi Smith wanted me to call him when I got in, didn't matter how late.

I dialed and waited through six or seven rings.

"Yeah?"

"Jimmi?"

"Lew. Thanks for calling me back. You found out anything?"

"Not much. Not as much as I would've hoped for. But I do have a good lead and something may come of that. I'll let you know."

"Yeah, please do, and Lew—?"

"Yeah."

"Thanks. You're a good man, don't ever let no one tell you different from that."

"Good night, Jimmi."

I walked into the bathroom. Vicky was reading a novel; only her head and hands and two small knee-islands stuck out above water. I lifted her glass off the side of the tub and took a sip of brandy.

"Any calls for me?" she said.

I shook my head. "You want company?"

"This tub's not big enough for the both of us, partner."

"I'll take one of Alice's pills and make myself small."

"O well. Perhaps the water will shrink you."

She raised her knees and patted the water in front of her: "Right here, cowboy."

Afterwards, just as we were drifting off to sleep, I asked her, "How many units would your head nurse assign to *that?*"

"*Grrrrr,*" she told me.

Since Vicky was going back on nights, we had a rare, leisurely breakfast together the following morning, stretching it out, over coffee, fruit, toast, boiled eggs and herring, to well over an hour. She had decided that she fancied a bit of shopping this morning. We rinsed and stacked dishes, and I dropped her off on Canal on my way to the loan company.

There wasn't much, and what there was, was lightweight. I spent a few hours chasing leads around the downtown area and netted enough to call it a day (a *slow* day, mind you), then remembered that I'd forgotten to drop off the extra twenty I had promised Kirk Woodland and headed back out to Metairie.

A squad car sat outside Baker's house and a cop opened the door when I knocked.

"What's your business?" the cop said. He'd recently grown a mustache to make him look older. It hadn't helped.

"Mr. Griffin. How did you know?" Baker said from across the room.

"You know this man?" Mustache said.

"A friend," Baker said, and asked me again how I knew. Mustache stepped back and let me walk in.

"I didn't," I said. "Don't. I was passing by and saw the chariot."

"Denny's disappeared, Mr. Griffin. Nothing like this's ever happened before. I went around the corner for some milk and when I got back, he was gone. He *never* left the house when I wasn't here."

"He probably didn't go very far, Mr. Baker. He'll turn up soon. You have my number. Call if there's anything I can do to help."

"I hope you're right, Mr. Griffin. And thanks."

More from habit than anything else I took a few swings through the neighborhood. Seemed to be mostly older people, not many kids or much evidence of kids—swing sets, bicycles and the like.

There was a battered old gas station on one corner, the kind we used to hang around as kids, sharing precious bottles of Nehi and Pepsi, and I stopped there to fill up. Went into the cluttered, cavelike office to pay, half-blind in the dim light. A surprisingly young man sat between two room fans, sweating. I paid him, looked around at the cheesecake calendars and asked if by any chance he'd seen a kid go by in the last hour or two, a big kid.

Fear broke in his eyes.

"I ain't touched no kids in years. It ain't that I ain't had the need, but I done learned, I ain't going back inside for *nothing. You* guys gotta know I'm clean."

"Hey, take it easy."

He looked closely at me, squinting. "You ain't a cop?"

I shook my head.

"Look like one," he said.

"A friend up a few blocks, his son wandered off. Cops

are up there now. I thought maybe I could help, just look around some, at least."

"Wouldn't be that big, retarded kid?"

I nodded.

"Cops are up there now, they'll be down here soon enough."

"If you're clean, they won't bother you."

"Either I didn't hear that, or you just *look* black."

"Right," I said after a moment. "Something I heard Jack Webb say, I guess. Dumb. But good luck."

"Thanks. You too—finding the kid, I mean."

He shut off the fans and began counting the money in the register.

I made another couple of pointless swings around the neighborhood, started back into New Orleans, remembered I'd again forgotten to drop off the twenty at Woodland's, and turned around.

I was walking back to Woodland's when I heard something, or thought I did, in the apartment that had been Cherie's. I tried the door and it opened. Inside, Denny was sitting cross-legged in the center of the floor.

To this day I don't know how he found his way there or got the door open. But I took him home to his father, who insisted we have a drink together (cheap bourbon he probably kept under the sink and dipped into once a year for eggnog) and thanked me several dozen times. I walked back to the apartments—I'd forgotten the twenty again—then retrieved the car and pulled onto I-10 just in time to renew my acquaintance with five o'clock traffic, one of the best arguments there is against a steady job.

I turned on the radio, listened to six tunes and moved ten feet. There was a new cold front coming through, due to hit about midnight. Some guy down in Austin had killed his neighbors' barking dog, invited them over for dinner, and served "a delicious stew."

Traffic eventually untangled, and I got home around six-thirty. Vicky had curried a chicken, marinated some raw vegetables and made trifle. Afterwards we sat for a long time over coffee. Vicky was talking about things she'd seen in the hospital, on the streets.

"There's something centrally wrong here, something hard and unyielding," she said. "I feel it in so many of the people I have as patients and I see it in the eyes of people who drive past me in their cars. It's li'l wonder so many of you are half crazy. Not just dotty, mind you, but wild—driven. I don't see how a foreigner could ever feel comfortable here, could ever fit in. I don't see how *you* do."

"I haven't, for much of my life, Vicky. You know that."

She poured more coffee for us both and we sat a while in silence. Outside, wind nudged at the building the way a dog does, with its head, when it wants to be petted.

"Would'ya come back to Europe with me, Lew?"

It was certainly a new idea, something I'd never thought of, and I gave it due consideration before shaking my head. Thinking of all those blues- and jazzmen, of Richard Wright, Himes, Baldwin. "I'd feel more the outsider there than you do here. America is something I have to deal with, however and in whatever ways I can, something I can't run away from."

"Things are so different there."

"I know."

She nodded. "Henry James said somewhere, 'It's a complex fate, to be an American.'"

"Was that before or after he became, to all intents and purposes, British?"

She laughed. "Quite."

Later, lying beside her, I wanted to ask her not to leave me, not to go back. I wanted to say that my time with her was the best I'd ever had, that through her I felt connected to humanity, to the entire world, as I had never felt before; that she had saved my life; that I loved her. There was so *much* I wanted to say, and never had or would.

Chapter Five

About nine-thirty Vicky got up, showered and started dressing. I lay in bed watching her pull on white stockings, creased slacks, uniform top. There's something about all that white, the way it barely contains a woman, its message of fetching innocence and concealment, that reminds us how much we remain impenetrable mysteries to one another. We circle one another, from time to time drawing closer, more often moving apart, just as we circle our own confused, conflicting feelings.

After she was gone I got up, poured half a glass of scotch and, still naked, switched on the TV. It was on the PBS channel from an opera we'd watched a week or so back. A young white guy in corduroy coat, chambray work-shirt and steel-rim glasses was talking about the blues.

"Because the slave could not say what he meant," he was saying, "he said something else. Soon he was saying all sorts of things he didn't mean. We'd call it dissembling. But what he *did* mean, that was the blues."

An old sepia of Dockery Plantation came on-screen.

"Much of what we know about early country blues centers about this Mississippi farm. And from here came the first of the *magic* names in country blues—Charley Patton."

Photo of Patton, pompadour hair, Indian cheek-bones, Creole skin. In the background, "Some Of These Days."

Patton's photo giving way to an artist's sketch of Robert Johnson and "Come In My Kitchen."

Bessie Smith and "Empty Bed Blues," Lonnie Johnson, Bukka White and Son House, Sonny Boy Williamson's "Been So Long" with mournful, sobbing harmonica over a vocalized bass line.

"Big Joe Williams." Full screen, then quarter screen above and to the left of Corduroy Steel-rim. "He once told an interviewer that all these young guys had it wrong. They were trying to get inside the blues, he said, when what the blues was, was a way of letting you get *outside*— outside the sixteen or eighteen hours you had to work every day, outside where you lived and what you and your children had to look forward to, outside the way you just plain *hurt* all the time."

Very low behind him, some sprightly finger-picked ragtime from Blind Blake, segueing into Blind Willie Johnson's "Dark Was The Night."

"Blues, then, developed, ultimately, as another form of dissembling, another way of not saying what was meant. As a 'safe' way of dealing with anger, pain, disillusion, rage, loss. The bluesman singing that his baby's done left him again is not talking about the end of a relationship, he is bemoaning the usurpation of his entire life and self."

I shut the TV off, poured more scotch and tried to think what it would be like without her. Stepped out onto the balcony to watch the parade of scrubbed and scruffy souls in the street below. The combination of cold without, and warmth within from whiskey, was exhilarating, electric. Tomorrow would bring good things. Vicky would not leave.

I had just turned the TV back on (a jungle movie) when the phone rang. It was Sansom, wanting to know if I'd heard from Jimmi recently.

"Last night. Any particular reason?"

"He didn't come back to the house after work tonight. An hour or so ago I called the day care center. He never showed up there today. I've got some people out asking questions."

"I hope they get answers."

"He seem upset when you talked to him, Lew?"

"No. Calm, really. Just wanted to know if I'd turned up anything."

"Had you?"

"Not really. A place she used to visit a retarded kid is all. Odd, though: the kid ran away today, too."

"Something in the air."

"Them Russians, maybe. Or fluoride—yes, senator?"

"I s'pect so. But my record stands. I have voted against Russians, sin and fluoride ever since I been put in this office by the good people 'f Loose-e-ana."

Then he was serious again.

"You'll let me know if you hear anything, Lew?"

"You've got it."

"Good man. How's it all going?"

"Okay. Vicky may go back to Europe."

"Yeah? You going with her?"

"I don't think so."

"Ought to consider it. Things are different over there. Gotta go, Lew. People with problems. Later."

Onscreen, native porters had fled the safari in terror, scattering their baskets and knapsacks on the ground. Bwana fired a shot into the air and shouted at them in pidgin English.

A few minutes later Vicky called to say good night and to tell me it was a madhouse down there. "And the night's just starting up," she said.

I turned the TV off (elephants, lions and snakes) and went back to bed but couldn't sleep. Got up and drew a tub of water. Too many things stomping, prowling and slithering in my mind.

An hour or so later I awoke, up to my neck in cold water.

I pulled the plug, toweled off and had another shot of scotch. It was almost two o'clock. My head hit the pillow already dreaming.

In the morning there was light, lots of it, and red hair, lots of that too. Then Vicky's face close to mine: "Rise and shine. Or at very least, rise. Up. Daytime. Work. Remember?"

"This the way you treat your patients?"

"You don't know?"

Still in her whites, she lay down alongside me. On the pocket of her uniform top there was a large yellow-orange stain, a starlike sprinkle of blood spots across the front of it.

"Forget work. Stay here with me."

"Bad night?"

"Everything it promised to be and more."

"Maybe you should be thankful. Few things *are* what they promise, these days."

She nuzzled into me, took a deep breath and said, "We had a cop come in tonight, Lew. Some gang had suckered him into an alley, kids, all of them. They closed him off, beat him and took his gun, then every one of them buggered him. When they were done with that, they slit him open like a pig, straight across the belly."

"You've seen worse."

"There was no reason for any of it. They weren't doing anything; he wasn't pursuing them. They didn't even know him. And someone else stood there behind a window and watched the whole thing happen before he even thought to call. What's wrong with this country, Lew?"

"I don't know. I've never known."

She sat up part way, leaning on an elbow.

"These last months, every time I hear a code called to ER I freeze up inside, something vital stops. I dream some days that I answer one of those calls and it's you there on the gurney, face rolling toward me."

"Everybody used to say my grandfather was too mean to die."

"But he did."

"He didn't seem very mean by then."

"We all die, Lew. Good, cruel or indifferent—and that's the most of us, I guess—we all die. Master and slave, elite and proletariat, elect and preterite alike. But no one should ever have to die like he did, in some filthy alley bleeding to death while the blokes who did it are standing over you laughing."

I held her for a long time then. And finally said, "I would have died if it hadn't been for you, Vicky. But you were there, and it was so very obvious that you cared. I'm sure I'm not the first one who's felt that way."

Tears runneled her cheeks. "And is that all we can do, Lew? Just ease another's pain, fluff a pillow, change the sheets, listen?"

"Is that so little?"

"No," she said, "of course not. But hold me, Lew."

Afterwards she fell asleep beside me, still in whites. I dozed off myself and woke ravenous.

I closed the blinds so she'd sleep on. Quietly found underwear, socks, shirt and suit, closed the bedroom door, opened it again and went back for belt and shoes. Showered, shaved and dressed. Then went into the kitchen for a breakfast (or lunch perhaps, considering the hour) of leftover quiche and custard. During a second cup of coffee the phone rang and I jumped at it, trying to keep it from disturbing Vicky, overturning my chair. It was Manny from the loan company, wanting to know if I was coming in today.

"Got a stack of 'em, Lew."

"Sorry. Overslept. Give me twenty minutes—fifteen if there's a tailwind."

As I was leaving, Vicky opened the bedroom door.

"Be careful, Lew," she said.

There was, indeed, a stack of them. I sorted through, first picking out names I knew from other times—those were usually quick collections, all you had to do was show up—then the ones close-in to town. After thirty minutes or so I figured I had a week's work and told Manny so.

"So? Anybody else we've had, it would be *three* weeks' work. There's a few would have fainted or run home to mama at the prospect. Get out of here, Lew, and don't come back till you're ready to."

"With the cash, of course."

"Or some reasonable facsimile."

"Thanks, Manny."

I was almost out the door when he said, "I hear your woman's leaving you, Lew."

"Maybe. How'd you know?"

He shrugged and splayed his fingers against the desktop. "People talk. It gets 'round. You know." He looked up from the desk, eyes huge behind glasses. "She's pretty special, huh?"

"Aren't they all?" Then, ashamed, "Yes. She is."

"Good luck, Lew. I hope it works out good for you, you deserve it."

"Thanks. Hey, can I go get your money now?"

"Absolutely. Mine and anyone else's you happen to come across. Wouldn't think of stopping you."

I put in a solid ten hours. The overall take was $4,617. Manny got forty percent of recovery. My own commission was ten percent of Manny's cut. Short primer in capitalism.

Vicky was already at work when I got home. She'd left a note on the fridge: *Great morning. I missed you tonight. Sleep well. Ta.* In the oven she'd left a casserole; a bowl of soup was atop the stove, fresh bread wrapped in a warm towel nearby.

On the bedside table I found the book she was currently reading. Stiff yellow cover with title and author in black, no blurbs or jacket illustrations. I opened it at random and read, translating word-by-word as I went along:

"Though it was only an Autumn Sunday, I had been born again, life lay intact before me, for that morning, after a parade of temperate days, there had occurred a cold fog not clearing until almost midday; and a change in the weather is sufficient to create the world and ourselves anew."

If only that were true, I thought. If *anything* were sufficient to create the world and ourselves anew.

I remembered, only a few months ago, walking along the river with the words *tabula rasa* and *palimpsest* rolling about in my mind.

But the world doesn't change, and mostly we don't

either, we just go on looking into the same mirror, trying on different hats and expressions and new sets of vice, opinion and prejudice; pretending, as children do, to see and feel things that are not there.

Like most small Southern towns, the place I was born and grew up in had its share of drunks. Lots of folks drank, some heavily, but of them all—those who agelessly, perpetually stumbled and raged along the streets (dirt for many years, then gravel, eventually blacktopped); others in clothes just as threadbare though aggressively clean, who were themselves pie-eyed most weekends and evenings—of them all there was one that everybody talked about. Almost as though this were an elected, honorary position, or something like the African *griots*, mavericks central to their culture yet reviled. *Griots* in Senegambian society sang the praises of their social leaders, committed to memory epic genealogies which became the oral history of their culture, sang and played in groups to set rhythms for farmers and others at their work. Yet when the *griot* died he could not be buried among his society's respectable folk. His body, instead, was left to rot in a hollow tree.

The one everybody in my town talked about was a barber, "a damned good barber" they would say, shaking their heads, "if he could just leave that bottle alone." (Others added: "And that pussy.") I grew up playing with his son, Jerry—a schoolteacher now—because we both lived way outside town, and the black-white line blurred as you got farther out. Neither of us had much of anyone else to play with.

Anyhow, one day Jerry's dad came home from the shop stone-sober and said he was going away for a while to think things over. He stuffed some jeans and T-shirts and a few flannels into paper bags. On the kitchen table he left a stack of money, payment he'd received from selling his shop and (apparently) money that he'd hoarded all those years when everyone was saying he'd spend his last cent on drink. It was (Jerry told me all this much later) an amazing sum of money. And that was the last time he saw his father.

His father moved into a cave out by the lake and lived there for years, but Jerry would never go see him. He lived off what he could forage from the woods and fish caught from the lake, never again coming into town. A lot of people said he had finally cracked up. Others went to him for advice.

In my junior year of high school I discovered books: Thoreau, then rather quickly people like Gandhi, Tolstoy, Twain, Faulkner. Devoured whole biographies of them and their own books the way other kids did candy or sandwiches, spent days hunched over their letters and diaries in that drifting Delta dust, my spine an oversize question mark.

Hobbes, for instance, with his paradox of power. The more power one had, Hobbes said, the more power it took to maintain that power. Only when you were truly a nobody, when you had nothing anyone could possibly want, were you free to be left alone and to go on about the tiny business of your life undisturbed. I think Jerry's dad may have been aiming at something like that. And my people, Negroes, it came to me, were the ultimate Hobbesians.

None of that's very close to the truth, I suspect; part of it's what my youthful mind made (and wanted to make) of the scaffolding of facts, the rest of it what memory (forever more poet than reporter) has pushed into place. Probably Jerry's dad was just another drunk who went on one final, lifelong binge and dropped out (as they began saying a few years later) and finally drowned on his own vomit or in the lake's slimy, sulphurous water. Anyhow, in college I used that story for a couple of English and history themes, and for my term paper in philosophy, and always got A's.

I don't know what time I at last fell asleep, but it seemed I had just done so when the phone rang.

"I'm sorry to wake you, but I was afraid otherwise you might worry."

I looked at the clock. It was a little before seven. Outside, birds were tuning up.

"I'm going to stay over a bit, if that's all right. We've had a bad night and now three call-ins, all RN's. I just can't leave the girls with all this. Are you going in today?"

"Maybe not. Had a good day yesterday. I'll see."

And went immediately back to sleep, waking only when Vicky climbed into bed beside me.

"I'm so very tired," she said. Then: "But not *that* tired."

Afterwards I looked at the clock again—a bit afternoon— and eased myself out of bed. Vicky turned onto her left side and mumbled. I heated water, ground some beans, shaved, then came back, dressed, and took the coffee out onto the balcony.

People swirled and plunged toward their work like water rushing down a drain. How many lived the same life for forty years: up at six, shower at six-fifteen, breakfast, second coffee, seeing kids off to school, on the interstate or St. Charles or bus or trolley by eight, at the office or store by nine? Then home by six, a drink or two, dinner, TV or games with the kids maybe, out to the mall on Mondays or Thursdays, a movie or ball game Sunday afternoon?

I had a son. It had been a long time since I'd seen him, since I'd wanted to see him. I wanted to see him now. But then Walsh called.

"Lew? Didn't think I'd catch you in. I was just talking to Bill Sansom. Jimmi Smith's been hurt, he's pretty bad. Sansom said you'd want to know about it."

"What happened, Don?"

"He was jumped by a gang of some kind, apparently. Beat him with something, chains or tire irons, maybe. Stabbed him a couple of times. Got one lung."

"Any idea why?"

"You know as well as I do that there doesn't have to be a reason. Probably isn't. Just he was there."

Don turned away from the phone, spoke to someone, listened, spoke again.

"Gotta go, Lew. Jimmi just arrested. They're losing him."

Chapter Six

THING WAS, YOU could tell the guy cared. Thirty years riding herd on this zoo, living in muck and mire like a catfish, and he could still be concerned about a small-time sex offender doing his damndest to make good.

When I got to the hospital—Don hadn't told me where he was and I'd had to call around—he met me in the lobby. "Let's go get drunk, Lew," he said. So we did.

It had been a long time for both of us. We started at Kolb's with dark German beer and drank our way purposefully into the Quarter. We were sober and depressed for hours, then suddenly drunk and afloat. By the time the suit people began their five o'clock hegiras homeward we were stewing in our own juices in the far corner of a bar on Esplanade, doe-eyed bartender and teenage transvestite our sole compatriots.

"You gon' be able t'drive, Lew?" Walsh said.

"Sure. But if I drive, *you* gotta find the car."

"S'only fair."

But he couldn't and I couldn't either, and after an hour

or so of trying we walked back to Café du Monde. Stuffed doughnuts into our mouths and washed them down with chicory coffee until the world slowed, shuddered and stood still again.

"It's still by the hospital, in the lot," Don said. "The car."

"Right. One more for the road?"

He ordered another coffee for each of us, and I went inside to phone Vicky.

By this time it was almost ten, and she was getting ready for work. "I was worried, Lew," she said. I briefly told her what had happened and said I'd be home soon. "Be careful, Lew," she said, "I'll leave some food on the stove for you."

What she left was sweet potatoes, grits and pork chops, all obviously ready some hours ago—food I'd grown up eating, wholly alien to her. I wondered if she had found a cookbook somewhere (*were* there cookbooks for this stuff?) or talked to my mom. Whatever, she'd taken some trouble. I tried to get her at the hospital and was told she was tending to an emergency.

I was almost asleep when she called back.

"I've got two minutes between the elevator-case stabbing and the MI on its way from Freret," she told me.

"Soul food?" I said. "What's that in French?"

"It's our anniversary, Lew. I wanted to do something a bit special."

"You *are* special, Vicky. You don't have to do anything special."

"The MI's here now, Lew; I have to go. I'll see you in

the morning. Perhaps we could have breakfast out; I'd like that."

"I would too."

Quiet then; the shush of the air-conditioner, the humming in wires. Far off a radio plays early rock and roll. I try to juggle my memories and what I am, and the two do not get along. They come together at the rim of a mountain, circling one another, snarling, flashing teeth. There are dark clouds and lightning to the south. Now it is light—it could be seven, or eleven—and Vicky is beside me.

We missed breakfast. Sometime in early afternoon the phone gradually penetrated my sleep but whoever it was didn't stay around long enough for me to answer. I turned on the answering machine and went back to bed. At five or so we roused, showered, and read the *Times-Picayune* over cups of cappuccino at a neighborhood Italian restaurant. There wasn't much in the paper; the real day's news came from Vicky.

"I turned in my notice this morning, Lew."

"I see. Then . . ."

She nodded. "Won'tya reconsider, Lew? Will you not come with me?"

"I can't," I said, noticing how manifestly my Southern *cain't* had shifted toward her own British *cahn't*.

"Then we'll have four good weeks together."

We hopped a cab to Commander's Palace for dinner, fresh trout for me, oysters in a red sauce for Vicky, and two bottles of wine, her departure growing between us like a wall of tall grass, something you try so hard not to mention that it enters every word and silence. We had brandy afterwards, then walked back over to St. Charles for the trolley.

It was filled with the usual collection of tourists, students, drunks, workers and quiet older folk who crossed themselves as we passed the churches. A pudgy, red-faced guy across the aisle kept staring over at Vicky and finally leaned toward us.

"I do hate to be a bother, but would you be British by any chance?"

"Je suis Française," Vicky said. *"Je ne parle pas anglais."*

He got off at Jackson Avenue, looking suspiciously back at us one last time.

"Wild boors," Vicky answered to my curious glance. "We breed them by the barrelful in Britain. One of the reasons I lived in France."

We'd got off at our own stop and started hiking across to the apartment, wind rising, cold air turning to crystal around us. We passed a young girl with a baby buggy (*pram,* Vicky would have said) full of groceries, a group of Spanish-speaking middle-aged men with guitars and accordions and a small, wood-frame harp. "I'm sorry, if that means anything," she said as we went in the front door, "and I'll miss you terribly, I'll miss you for a very long time, Lew." Then later: "You're going to stay up?"

"A while."

"Will you wake me when you do come to bed, then?"

I nodded, knowing I probably wouldn't. She probably knew it too, hesitated and went away. I heard running water, the shower, toothbrushing, a clock being wound, classical music from the bedroom radio, turned low.

I poured brandy into a tea glass and watched the winking red eye of the telephone machine. Put on Bessie Smith and bobbed about for a while on the promise of her voice, on her empty bed blues, her nine-day crawl, her haunted house, on her thirst and her hunger. Every note and word was like something pulled with great difficulty from deep within myself.

"Cherie was here tonight," the answering machine told me when I finally got around to running the tape back and playing it. "This is Baker. Give me a call; I may have something for you."

I dialed and waited through a lot of rings. Looked at the clock: after midnight.

"Yes?"

"Mr. Baker. I'm sorry to wake you. Lew Griffin. I wasn't sure what you had could wait."

"Minute," Baker said at the other end. He put the phone down. I heard water running. Then he came back.

"It was about six or so. Heard a knock at the door, opened it, and there she was. Had a doll, some kind of dinosaur kind of thing, for Denny. Said she was sorry she hadn't got back sooner."

"How was she?"

"Looked good. Told me she'd been out of town, that things were looking up for her; she had a job and new friends, she said. I made her eat something—she's always been on the skinny side—and she and Denny spent an hour or maybe a little more together."

"She tell you anything about this job?"

"No. But as she was leaving she told me she wouldn't be able to come back again, that she was leaving town."

"And?"

He paused. "Cherie's been a good friend to us, to Denny and me. I'm not telling you this because she's a kid and we're big folks, or because you found Denny when he wandered off. I've thought about this a lot."

"Then why *are* you telling me?"

"I think because she told me three times, 'I'll be leaving for good on a Greyhound at two thirty-six this morning.' Almost like she wanted me, or someone, to stop her."

"Does she?"

"Who knows? I don't know what *I* want, most mornings. Maybe you could ask her."

"I could do that. Was she alone?"

"She came here alone, yes. After she left I looked out the window. A car pulled up to the curb a half-block up-town and she got in. A Lincoln, late model, dark."

"Thank you, Mr. Baker. Say hi to Denny for me."

"I will. And try to make Cherie understand why I had to tell you. She's a child, Griffin."

"Yes."

"Wonderful, but a child for all that."

"Sorry again to have waked you up."

"Believe me, I don't mind at all. One of the pleasures of my life is sitting alone here in the early morning with a cup of coffee, just looking out into the dark and thinking, remembering. I do it often. But not often enough."

I hung up to the sound of his teakettle whistling, walked into the bedroom and found Vicky fast asleep. Stretched out naked on the white sheets she looked almost like a child herself, pale and small, so vulnerable. Memories sprang into my mind like tigers.

I do it often, Baker had said, but not often enough.

And I realized how much of myself, of what I was now, was Vicky, the sound of her voice and those *r*'s, the books she read, her music, thin arms entering white sleeves, the sandals she wore in our hours together, her gentleness and curiosity. Whatever else should happen, all that would remain part of me forever.

I found a pad of paper and wrote on it slowly, haltingly: *Je t'aime toujours, et je te manquerai quand nous nous quittons. Longtemps je te manquerai.*

I tucked it underneath the clock she kept at bedside, one she'd had since nursing school. I could still hear that clock ticking as I walked out into the black, cold night, like a small heart, like a cricket, a needle stitching a life together, something that doesn't change.

Chapter Seven

TUCKED AWAY ANONYMOUSLY beneath an intersection of elevated expressways, the New Orleans Greyhound station resembles nothing so much as a bowling alley. It even smells like a bowling alley: sweat, sexual frustration, beer, piss, disinfectant, tobacco smoke, french fries, onion rings.

Cabs were stacked up at the exit, their drivers hunched over racing forms, newspapers or a game of craps on the sidewalk nearby. A tall black man in yellow kept watch over incoming buses and incoming youngish women. Inside I found the usual assortment of street people hoping for a warm place to sleep, guys and girls on the make for whatever the market might bear, teenage brides with kids in arm and tow, soldiers with duffel bags, dips and junkies, a few older couples visiting grown children or out to "see America." As I walked in one door a guy went through the plate glass of another door, pursued by two of the city's finest. No one paid them much attention.

Cherie was sitting in one of the back pews of plastic

chairs, eyes wide. A cheap brown suitcase and a huge shoulder bag were on the floor beside her. No one was in the next chair, so I took it. It was slick with sweat, beer, whatever.

"Hi," I said.

"Do I know you?" Eyes even wider.

"No, Cherie, you don't. But I'm a friend of your brother's, of Jimmi's, and I need to talk to you."

"How'd'ja know I was here?"

"Does it matter?"

After a moment she shook her head.

"Last night Jimmi was attacked by some hoods in the Quarter, some kind of youth gang apparently. They beat him up pretty bad and long. He's dead, Cherie. But before he died he'd asked me to find you for him. He was worried about you, and he loved you. I only wish I could have done it sooner, but I let my own life get in the way. I'm sorry for that. Jimmi was pretty special to me."

"To me, too," she said. "He was all I had, and I do thank you. But you'd best leave now, Mr.—?"

"Griffin. No, I don't think so."

It took about five minutes. I watched him stand up from his seat across the room, slowly make his way toward us. Six-four and muscles to match, wearing a polo shirt and white jeans with a tan linen sports coat, California hair.

"Pardon me, sir," he said. "But the lady *has* asked you to move along, I think."

"That's right."

"It really would be in both our interests if you would do so, sir."

"Probably so, otherwise you might have occasion to get your hair mussed. But not in the lady's, *n'est-ce-pas?*"

I looked up at him, half a mile at least, remembering Bible School stories of David and Goliath.

"I know you're a big, powerful man, sweetheart, and you're probably used to people trembling and maybe a few of them wetting their pants when you speak. The name's Lew Griffin. Maybe you should step out into the street and ask around before you do anything . . . precipitate?"

If he didn't buy the tough-guy act, maybe he'd think I was too smart to beat up.

"My employers will be most unhappy," he said after a moment.

"I certainly hope so."

"The girl's going with you, then?"

"Woman. If she wants to, yes."

We both looked at Cherie. She finally nodded.

"Perhaps we'll meet again," California said.

"Could be. I'll buy you a drink if we do."

"I don't drink. Destroys brain cells."

"*Vous avez raison. Quand vous avez si peu . . .*"

"What's that?"

"Just agreeing with you is all."

"Yeah," he said. "Yeah, sure. Well, take care, Lew Griffin."

"Always have."

He turned and walked through the now glassless door,

ducking low. I saw him climb into a cab outside and wait until the driver looked up from the crap game and noticed he had a fare. The cab swerved out into traffic, sending a Cadillac into the next lane and into the path of a battered VW bus. Five minutes later, traffic was backed up half a mile or more.

We walked a couple of blocks over to the car and drove home. If she wondered where I was taking her, she didn't ask. Maybe she'd got used to letting other people make her decisions for her these past weeks. It was almost five as we turned onto St. Charles, and New Orleans was starting to show the first signs of day, like in horror movies when the corpse's hand begins to open and close there at the edge of the screen but no one notices.

Vicky was working a day shift. I showed Cherie the bathroom and spare bedroom and settled into the kitchen. Presently I heard the two of them talking. They came in together just as I slid the omelette out of the pan. Fruit was already sliced and arranged on another platter. I stacked toast on a saucer, poured coffee for us all, and brought warm milk to the table with me in its small copper pot.

We ate slowly, Vicky and Cherie talking for the most part, mostly about Vicky's work.

"I'd really like that, different all the time, meeting new people, really *doing* something," Cherie said.

"Well there's always a need for volunteers and nurses' aides, if you'd fancy that. You might be able to work your way into a regular job then."

"I'll have to just take whatever I can get, for now. I don't even know where I'm going to stay."

Vicky and I looked at one another.

"You're welcome to the spare bedroom here for as long as you need it," I said.

"Oh, I couldn't do that, Mr. Griffin."

"Lew."

"That's up to you, then," Vicky said. "But the room's here if you want it. It's never used."

"I know what it's like not to have anywhere or anyone to go to, Cherie; I've been there. Vicky knows too. She was raised in a French orphanage."

Cherie picked a grape out of the cluster at the center of the fruit plate.

"When we were growing up, our parents had this tiny little arbor in the backyard, just four whitewashed poles, some chicken wire and stakes, a few wild vines. There was a swing on the tree nearby, really a door Dad had hung with steel cable, and Jimmi and I'd sit at opposite ends of that swing eating grapes and spitting the seeds at each other. I haven't thought of that in a long time."

"I really must scoot on out of here," Vicky said. "Cherie, please feel free to help yourself to anything of mine that you might need. Are you going in to work today, Lew?"

"I'll catch some sleep first, I think, then see."

"Then I won't ring you. *Au revoir*."

She leaned down and touched my cheek with her own. I wondered what it would be like without her, what *I* would be like without her. It was a little like trying to imagine the world without trees or clouds.

"I'll clean up, Mr. Griffin."

"Lew. But I'll do it."

"I'd really rather have something to do, if you don't mind. You go on and get yourself some sleep."

"You're sure?"

She nodded.

"Then you've got it. Listen: for as long as you're here, this apartment is your own. Use what you need, come and go as you please, if you can't find something, ask. Do you need money?"

"I have . . . an advance, from the people I was going to work for."

"Okay, then. Goodnight, Cherie."

"Goodnight, Lew. *Bon soir*—is that right?"

"As rain."

I showered and lay listening to the distant clatter of pans and dishes, the irregular rush of water. My childhood rose up around me: myself tucked away in bed while, as on a far-off planet, family life continued.

Soon dishes and kitchen were done and I heard the TV come on. Some vague news about an arms talk, I think; premonitions of continued cold weather; a human interest story about twins in Poland and Gary, Indiana. An old movie with zombies, diplomats, displaced Russian aristocrats, rutting teenaged Americans.

I fell asleep and at some later point woke to the sound of sobbing. Walked into the living room and found a talk show and Cherie asleep on the couch, half-nude, dreaming. Felt the gulf between us, and felt my own loneliness in a way I'd not done for some time.

She was sobbing somewhere deep inside the dream. I think for a moment I felt as parents feel, wanting to protect her at any cost, to lie or tell her whatever might calm her sleep, ease her waking. But parents, most parents, learn that can't be done. They learn that, whoever we are, all we can really share is the common humanity that bonds us: the knowledge that we *all* hurt, that every choice is difficult and, in its own way, final.

I fetched some blankets from the closet and covered her, turned the TV off, returned to bed.

Either it's only in the relationships we manage that we live at all, or we must think that in order to manage them in the first place. We go on trying not just to survive, but to find reasons, such as love, that allow us to betray ourselves into *choosing* survival.

In my dreams Martin Luther King was reading *Black No More*. Tears streamed down his face: rain on a window behind which there is laughter.

At some point Vicky was there, muttering something about croissants; then, later, we were making love, and later still (I think) there was somehow coffee beside the bed. Gradually I was awake and it was dark. I thought how recent days were like older ones, going by in a blur, undistinguished, largely unlived, so many twilights retreating into bleary dawns.

Finally a knock at the door, repeated twice.

"There's dinner, when you want it." Footsteps leaving.

We showered together and went to see.

A stew of chicken and vegetables, spinach tossed with egg and vinaigrette, pasta salad, fried bananas. Freshly ground coffee after.

"This time *I* do the dishes," I said.

And did so, listening to the chirr of their conversation in the next room. Vicky had spoken with the head of volunteer services and the nursing director; both wanted to see Cherie for interviews.

I remembered Jimmi sitting up in bed without clothes reading *Principles of Economy*, thought of the first time I saw Vicky, just so much red hair floating above me, of how Cherie had looked so very young in the photograph and (as Vicky said) like someone who knows the best part of her life is already over. Maybe the best parts of our lives are *always* over.

Maybe happiness, contentment, are things we only recollect through the filters of time, elusive ghosts forever behind us.

In the next room they laughed together, Vicky's an easy, rolling laugh, Cherie's curiously childlike, and I thought: that's really the only answer we have, laughter. For a long time after it was over I stood listening.

Chapter Eight

A FEW WEEKS later Vicky and I were standing together at New Orleans International. The weather had gone suddenly, unseasonably warm. We watched a small private plane gather speed and tear itself away from the earth. Earlier Don, Sansom and some others had been over for drinks and good-byes. Now it was our turn.

"I don't know what might make you happy, Lew," she said, "But whatever it is, I hope you'll find it."

"Or give up trying?"

"Quite." She put her hand over mine on the railing. We could feel the heat through the window. I would never forget her eyes, the way her mouth shaped itself around words as they left it. "You didn't know, but when I met you I had decided already to leave, to go home. I was never certain why I didn't, not until you came to Hotel Dieu and found me. Only then did I realize that was what I had waited for."

"I was in pretty terrible shape when you met me, Vicky."

"Aren't we all . . . You know where I'll be, Lew. You can come anytime, if you change your mind."

"And you'll be waiting?"

"Waiting, no. But I will be there for you if you come. This has all been something very special for me, Lew." She held her hand up by her heart, closed, then slowly opened it.

Eventually her flight was called, we fumbled through final farewells and awkward embraces, and she followed the laws of perspective down an embarkation tunnel.

I went to the bar for a drink and ran into a guy I'd gone to high school with and hadn't seen since. Vicky had sold the car just before leaving. He was a cabbie now and offered me a free run home. But when we walked out a couple of hours and several drinks later, there was Verne leaning against the streetlight at the corner.

"Need a ride home, soldier? I've got my car."

"I hope you don't mind, Lew," she said, feinting her way onto the expressway. "I know what just went down. Thought you could use a friend about now."

"And always. But what about your doctor?"

She shrugged. "History."

I watched her face pass through lights like a boat over waves.

"Are you okay?"

"Fine," she said. "I've kept up, Lew. I talked to Don Walsh and some others, I always knew how you were, what you were up to."

"You should have called. Or just come by."

She shook her head. Several blocks passed beneath us as we curved across the city's sky.

"Are you working?"

"Yeah," she said, and laughed. "At a rape crisis center—can you feature that? For a long time now."

"You get paid?"

"Sometimes."

A little later she looked over at me and said, "Where'll it be, Lew?"

"I don't want to go back to my place."

"I thought you might not. There's always mine."

"Catching balls on the rebound?"

She shrugged. "Whatever works. You wait and see."

"Right," I said. "You wait and see."

Part Four 1990

Chapter One

I STILL HEAR from Vicky, almost every month: long, chatty letters about what she's doing, new friends and books, seeing *The Big Sleep* for the first time in Paris, discovering Faulkner, a trip to Russia. She even went back for a visit to the orphanage where she grew up. Still moving through the world with eyes wide, holding on to every fugitive moment of it.

Cherie had started working full time as a nurse's aide just before Vicky left, and took over the apartment lease. Then she worked her way through nursing school. I don't hear from her too often, but she's doing fine—nice home outside Lake Charles, a hardworking guy who loves her, two kids that look a lot like Jimmi in the photos she sends every Christmas. At least for Cherie, the best part *wasn't* over.

I stayed at Verne's a few weeks, moved out to a furnished room (mutual decision), moved back in (mine). I was getting ready to move out again (we got along great as long as we didn't live together) when I had an accident—the accident consisted of turning my back on a guy I'd just

leaned on, hard, for money he owed the loan company—
and Verne said: Don't be silly, stay here.

For a while, in short, life was as complicated as that
sentence you just read.

Laid up in bed with a concussion and cracked ribs,
more or less just to relieve boredom, I wrote a book called
Skull Meat, about a Cajun detective in New Orleans. Just
lay there and spun it out, making it up out of whole cloth,
improvising wildly, throwing in whatever came to me. The
publisher paid me three thousand for it. Then, when it sold
okay, he offered me five thousand to do another with the
same character, and that one took. We got reviews in major
papers, foreign sales, even a movie option. (The books are
very popular in France, Vicky tells me.) Some critics
started talking about me in the same sentence as Chandler,
Hammett, Macdonald and Himes; they shouldn't have,
because those guys are way out of my league, but they did.

I don't make a lot of money really, but with a book every
year or so I'm able to pay the rent, buy what I need, stay
out of debt and off the streets.

You write three or four hours, which is about all you can
handle and stay sane, and then there's still most of the day
ahead of you. I tried reading Proust and the whole of
Chekhov, awful TV movies, afternoon matinees at two
dollars, avocational drinking. Finally I signed up for
courses at Dillard and finished my B.A. Now I teach one
or two days a week, just filling in, French mostly, an occa-
sional writing course. I do it mainly because it's fun, not
for the money, and I learn far more than any of my

students. As you get older you need some way of staying in touch with the young, something to keep your head working and turning, something to plow uprooting presumptions, new faces, new crops.

Verne and I found an old house just outside the Garden District with a slaves' quarters behind, and that's where I work. I have a stereo and lots of blues records out here, a filing cabinet, a desk with cubbyholes, another desk for the typewriter, a few books, and not much else. Roaches, of course. I turn on lights at night and the desks go from black to white.

I was eighty pages into a new novel, *The Severed Hand*, wondering if my crazy Cajun was about to beat someone up or *get* beaten up in a bar scene. I had on Cajun music as I often did while writing these books, hoping that wild, droning pulse might somehow work its way into what I was writing. Nathan Abshire sawed away at "Pinegrove Blues" on his accordion, a song he recorded under various names, at least once as "Ma Négresse." I looked back through the manuscript and found that Boudleaux had been beaten up two chapters ago, so I figured it was time for him to win one. A character in the book was pretty clearly based on Blaise Cendrars—hence the title. I wondered if any reviewers or critics would pick up on that. I also wondered if other writers (because I didn't know any) played such games to get themselves through their books.

The phone rang and went unanswered for some time, so Verne had to be out. I picked it up, leaning over to lower the volume of the music (*felt* more than heard now) and said "Yes?"

"Lew? Jane." A brief pause. "Janie."

The past leapt like a toad into my face.

"I'm very sorry to bother you, and I know you'd probably rather hear from just about anybody else but me. But I was wondering when you last heard from David."

"Three, four months at least. A postcard with bored-looking gargoyles; he was in Paris. The back of it was covered with that tiny handwriting of his, all about people he'd met, things and places he'd finally seen after reading about them for so long. He was even thinking about staying on in Europe once his sabbatical was done."

"And nothing since?"

"Nothing."

"Is that usual? I mean, I don't know how regularly you two traded letters after you started keeping up with each other."

"Not *un*usual, at any rate. Several months of absolute silence, then a ten-page letter; that seemed often to be the pattern between us."

I reached over and turned the music off. A grasshopper strolled obliquely across the outside of my window, legs finding no difficulty with the smooth glass.

"I assume that something's wrong, Janie, else you wouldn't have called me, not after all these years."

"I don't know, Lew. That's the worst part. But David wrote me almost every week, on Sundays usually, and I haven't heard anything now for over two months."

"Where is he supposed to be?"

"Somewhere between Rome and New York."

"You have an address for him?"

"The last one was just *poste restante* to a post office in Paris. He was supposed to let me know."

"Seven-five-oh-oh-six?"

"Yes."

"That's the same one I have, then. Have your letters been returned?"

"No."

"Then he, or at least someone, is probably getting them. Or forwarding them, anyhow."

"Someone?"

"Janie. It's probably nothing; you know that."

"Yes. But I have bad feelings about it. And it's halfway across the world, Lew, almost like another planet. I had to call you, to talk to someone. It took a long time to get up enough courage."

"You don't talk to your husband?"

"My husband stopped listening years ago. More recently, he stopped being here. There's a number I can call if I absolutely *have* to see him about something."

"And you accept that?"

"Like I have a choice? I'm probably still nineteen or twenty to you, Lew, young, attractive—attractive as I ever was, at least. But the truth is I'm almost fifty and can't think of much reason to get out of bed most mornings. I'm fat, my hair's falling out, my teeth are awful. I was never really pretty. Now I'm worse than plain. No man can ever know what that means."

"Maybe a man who's loved you can. Give me a number."
She did. "It may be a while."

The grasshopper had completed its tour and disappeared. I walked out into sunlight and sat on a bird-bespattered bench under one of the trees. Slowly sunlight gave way to evening. Slowly the toad became only history, and bearable.

Chapter Two

I WENT INSIDE and called Columbia University, reaching the English department without *too* much trouble (after all, in most universities we're dealing with bureaucracies aspiring to heights achieved only in the Soviet Union), finally getting through to the chairman.

"Yes?" he said. "Could I help you?" in an accent that was part New England, part Virginia. The sort of accent you think of Robert Lowell as having.

I told him who I was and asked if David was safely back at work.

"As a matter of fact, Mr. Griffin, we're quite worried about Dave up here. He was to have been on campus last week, and should *en effet* have met his first class today. But no, we've heard nothing. He's not there, by any chance?"

"No. There's been no word from him—no one he was close to, to whom he might have sent a postcard, a letter?"

"Well, of course we all like him a great deal. Admire his work tremendously, it goes without saying. But *close*, no. I don't think so. Not very social, Dave, if you know what I mean. Keeps his own counsel. Different drummers and all that. But wait, now that I think of it, there *was* one of the librarians he saw quite often, Miss Porter, our special collections curator. Nothing of the romantic sort, you understand, but good colleagues. Would you like me to transfer you? Miss Porter should be on duty?"

"If you don't mind."

"Not at all, *es nada*. By the way, I'm a great admirer of yours. We've even taught your books, in a course we offered on the proletarian novel, quite a *popular* course as it turned out."

"Thank you. I've always thought of them as only entertainment."

"Ah. And so they are, most decidedly. But on another level certainly a bit more than mere entertainment—no?"

"Maybe."

"That's the stuff: keep the critics guessing, eh? Here you go then, over to Special Collections."

I got an idiot undergrad shelver, with persistence a graduate assistant, and finally Miss Porter, who told me to call her Alison, one *l*. She said it as though no one ever had. I explained who I was.

"I thought maybe you'd have had a card, a letter. We don't even know if he's back in the States," I said.

"Well," she said. "He did write almost every week. We have so much in common, you know. I'm a real Francophile; and he would write and tell me all his discoveries, all about the people he'd met, rare books or manuscripts he had seen all over France. I so looked forward to those letters."

"When did you last hear from David, Miss Porter—Alison?"

"O dear, I really wouldn't know. Time and dates and those things just get terribly away from me. Could you hold a moment?"

I said certainly, and listened to the humming in the wires.

"Yes, here it is. The last letter I have is dated 24 August, from Paris. Then there's a postcard, no return address but with a New York postmark, the date on it's something of September—seventh, seventeenth? Just 'See you soon, *amitiés*.'"

"And nothing since?"

"*Rien*."

"Thank you, Alison. I hope if you have further word you'll let us know." I gave her my number, thanked her again, and hung up.

After a while I went across the patio into the house and put on the kettle. I was grinding beans when the front door opened and, a little later, Verne came into the kitchen.

"Coffee, huh?"

"Right."

"Enough for me?"

"Always."

She filled a pitcher and started watering plants on the window ledge.

"Gonna be away a few days, Lew."

"Milk?"

"Black, I think. You be okay?"

"As always."

We sat at the kitchen table, steaming cups between us. Verne sipped and made a face.

"You're not angry with me."

I shrugged.

"You know I'll always come back. No one else makes coffee like you."

She took her cup and drank it while packing. I turned on the radio to *The Marriage of Figaro*. Later I heard the cab driver at the door, Verne's suitcase bumping against the sill as she left. And then the silence.

Chapter Three

THAT NIGHT, SUDDEN and unseen in the embracing dark, as though the city, like Alice, had tumbled into some primordial hole and through to another world, a storm broke.

I woke, at three or four, to the sound of tree limbs whipping back and forth against the side of the house. Power had summarily failed, and there were no lights, was no light, anywhere. Wind heaved in great tidal waves out there in the dark somewhere. Rain hissed and beat its fists against the roof. Yet looking out I could see nothing of what I sensed.

It went on another hour, perhaps more, the edge, as we learned the next day, of hurricanes that touched down in Galveston, extracting individual buildings like teeth, and blew themselves out on the way up the channel toward Mobile.

The morning we learned this, weather was mild, air exceptionally clear, sun bright and cool in the sky. Worms had come out onto sidewalks and lay there uncurled in the steam rising lazily from them. In every street, cars maneuvered around the fallen limbs of age-old trees. And ship-wrecked on the neutral ground, crisscrossing trolley tracks, lay uprooted palms—fully a third of the city's ancient, timeless crop.

Chapter Four

AND IT SEEMED to them that in only a few more minutes a solution would be found and a new, beautiful life would begin; but both of them knew very well that the end was still a long, long way away and that the most complicated and difficult part was only just beginning.

I consoled myself with Chekhov.

Then I called David's number in New York and, getting no answer, dialed *O* and asked to be put through to a New York operator at that exchange. I got a quiet-spoken, courteous type and asked if it were possible to obtain the number of an apartment complex's superintendent in an emergency. She put me through to her supervisor, who listened to my explanation, said she'd call me back, did, and gave me the number for a Fred Jones.

I dialed again and got a "Yeah?"

"Is Mr. Jones in, please?"

"Depends. You a tenant?" In the background I could hear kids shouting one another down, a blaring TV.

"No ma'am," I said, hoping imagination might rush in, or at least stumble in, to fill the void.

"*About* one of the tenants, then."

"No ma'am."

"Yeah . . . Well, he's asleep, that's what it is. You want for me to wake him up?"

"I think that would be best, yes ma'am."

"He ain't gonna like it."

"Who does?"

A couple of minutes later I had Grizzly Jones on the line.

"New York P.D.," I told him. "We've got a missing-persons report down here, David Griffin, yours the last known address, hope you can help."

"Do all I can, officer. Always cooperate with the law. But we ain't seen him lately. Off to Europe, he tells us, this is back in June. I'm still picking up his mail out of the box. Apartment's paid up through November."

"Nobody living there?"

"No sir."

"You've been up there to check that personally?"

"A week ago. Part of what I'm paid for."

"You have the mail there by you?"

"Yeah, it's all here in a box, hold on a minute . . . Okay."

"Tell me what's there."

"The usual junk—bank statements, Mastercard bills, a few other charge cards, some magazines, a couple pounds of flyers and advertising. Schedule from a theater showing 'foreign and art' films. A book catalog from France."

"Nothing personal."

"No sir, not really."

"Thank you, Mr. Jones."

"Anytime, sir. Anything I can do for you, anything at all, you just call. You know?"

"I know. Good citizens like yourself make all our jobs easier."

"'s nothing."

He was right. It was *all* nothing.

(—I remind you of the curious incident of the dog in the nighttime.

—But the dog did nothing in the nighttime.

—That is the curious incident,

as my colleague Mr. Holmes once put it.)

I finished the pot of coffee, read a little more Chekhov, mixed a pitcher of martinis and dialed the transatlantic operator. Twenty minutes later I had Vicky on the line.

"It's so very good to hear from you. You're well, I hope."

"Ça va bien. Et tu?"

"Marvelous, especially now, talking to you again after all these years."

"They go by quickly, V."

"They do that, Lewis. And the people we care for and love go by almost as quickly."

"A lot of things have changed."

"A lot haven't."

"True enough. How's Jean-Luc?"

"Splendid. Translating computer books for the most part now. Boring, he says, but quite easy after all those lit'ry novels; and of course the pay's far, far better."

"And the real boss of the house?"

She laughed. "Yesterday in English class they had to write an essay: what I want to be when I grow up. Louis has assured us all, and in excellent English, that when *he* grows up, what he wants most is to be an American."

"In which case he'd better watch that excellent English."

"Quite."

"So he's in school already."

"Hard though it may be to believe. He's six, Lew."

"Really . . . Listen, I called to ask a favor of you."

"I can't think of anything you'd ask that I wouldn't gladly do."

"My son David has been in France this summer on sabbatical. We heard from him fairly regularly, his mother and I, I mean. Then it all stopped: letters, cards, everything. He hasn't shown up at his school though classes are underway. We don't even know if he's returned to the States."

"And you need for me to check over here?"

"Right. Whatever you can find out."

"I'll need return addresses, names of friends or university connections. What else? Airline credit cards?"

That was one *I* hadn't thought of. I gave her what I had, said the rest would be coming shortly by wire, including passport number. I thanked her.

"No thanks are necessry, Lew. When Louis grows up and becomes an American, you can track him down for me, tell him to write his poor mother."

"*Je te manque*, V."

"*Et moi aussi* . . . This may take a while, Lew. Things here in France aren't quite what they used to be."

"Are they anywhere?"

"*Au revoir, mon cher.*"

"*Au revoir.*"

I poured another glassful of martini and stepped out onto the balcony. New Orleans loves balconies—balconies and sequestered courtyards where you can (at least in theory) go on about your life at a remove from the bustle below and about you. Across the street, schoolgirls left St. Elizabeth's, every doubt or question anticipated, answered, in their catechism and morning instruction, strong young legs moving inside the cage of plaid uniform skirts.

Chapter Five

MY CAJUN, BLESS his ancient hunter's heart, was nosing closer and closer to the truth, improvising his way toward it the way an artist does, a jazz musician or bluesman, a poet, and I was remembering what Gide had said about detective stories in which "every character is trying to deceive all the others and in which the truth slowly becomes visible through the haze of deception." A few chapters back, I'd thrown in some passages from Evangeline, translated into journalese.

But something odd was occurring. The more I wrote about Boudleaux, the less I relied on imagination, using experiences and people of my own past, writing ever closer to my life. Now on page ninety-seven a red-haired nurse materialized without warning, tucking in the edges of Boudleaux's sheets (he'd been involved in a traffic accident) as she rolled her *r*'s. I figured Verne would be along soon, maybe even her latest exit scene.

I wrote till two or three that morning, weaving the nurse ever more tightly into the book's pattern, and fell

asleep finally on the floor when I lay down for a few minutes' break.

Sometime around dawn (I heard birds, and in half-light
could make out the phone's dim shape at the corner of the
desk) bells went off.

"Lew, I know it's quite early there . . ."

"I was almost up. Giving it serious consideration, anyway."

"*Voila*. Here it is, then. I've been 'round to the *pension*
where David was staying, and he left there, according to
plan, in late August, somewhere around the twenty-fifth,
giving his New York address for forwarding. Jean-Luc
rang up the travel agents and confirmed a reservation in
the name of David Griffin, departing Paris nonstop to
New York on the twenty-sixth, fare charged to David's
American Airlines card."

"Not bad for amateurs."

"The original meaning of amateur is someone who
cares, who loves, Lew. Is there anything more we can do
to help?"

"Not just now, but I can't say how much I thank you
both."

"You don't have to. *Ecris-moi, ou appelles-moi encore?*"

"*Bientôt, ma chère.*"

The connection went, leaving me alone there in the
rump end of America. I put on water for coffee, showered,
shaved and brushed my teeth, none of which helped much.
I ate a peach (thinking of Prufrock) and some scrambled
eggs. I lay down again, in a bed this time, and was almost
asleep when the phone rang.

"Lew? I'll be coming home tomorrow morning, if that's all right with you."

"I'll have breakfast ready," I said after a moment.

". . . I could come tonight. Or now."

"In that case *you* do breakfast." And fell back asleep, waking later to the smell of bacon, fresh coffee, hot grease, butter. It was dark outside, and I was disoriented. I walked out into the kitchen.

"Good whatever—morning? evening?" Verne said. "Have a seat and some coffee, not necessarily in that order."

I did, and while I drank she pulled skillets with omelettes and potatoes out of the oven, slipped buttered bread in to take their place, exhumed crisp bacon from layers of toweling. When the toast was done, she poured new coffee for me and a cup for herself, warm milk and coffee at the same time, New Orleans-style, and sat down across from me.

"How's the book going?"

"Slow as usual, but okay?" I said nothing about David, about Janie calling. "I may put you in it. Not you *really*, but someone like you."

"There *isn't* anyone like me, Lew."

I looked at her then, the way she held the toast, looking at it slightly cross-eyed, and I knew she was right. It's never ideas, but simple things, that break our hearts: a falling leaf that plunges us into our own irredeemable past, the memory of a young woman's ankle, a single smile among unknown faces, a madeleine, a piece of toast.

"I guess it'll have to be you, then," I said.

We finished the meal without talking. As Verne gathered up dishes, she said, "I'll be going after I've done these, Lew."

"But you just came back."

She shook her head. "A visit. That's all you allow, Lew. Whether years or a couple of days, always only a visit to your life." She began drawing water into the sink, squirted in soap. "You've never asked me to stay with you, not even for a night."

"But I always thought that should be up to you, V."

"'Up to you.' 'Whatever you want.' How many times have I heard that all these years—when I heard anything at all? Don't *you* want anything, Lew?" She turned from the sink, soapy water dripping onto the floor in front of her, hands curled back toward herself. She closed one hand and raised it, still dripping, to chest level. "I could be anyone as far as you're concerned, Lew—*any* woman." The hand opened. "People are interchangeable for you, one face pretty much like any other, all the bodies warm and good to be by sometimes."

She turned back to the sink, scrubbed at a plate. I took a towel from the drawer and stood beside her.

"In your books you never write about anything that's not past, done with, gone."

She handed me the plate, and she was right. I dried it. Put it in the rack at the end of the counter.

"Okay," I said, "but it doesn't make sense for you to leave. You stay here, keep the house, and I'll go."

She shook her head. "I'll stay with Cherie until I find a place. You do whatever you want to with the house and the rest."

We finished in silence, the past, or future, shouldering us quietly apart. I looked at the clock above the sink. It was 9:47. When Verne came back in to tell me she was leaving, it was 10:16.

Not too long after, the phone rang. I picked it up. "Yes?"

"Is La Verne there, please?" someone said after a moment's hesitation.

"No."

I hung up, turned off the light and sat staring out into the darkness. Somewhere in that darkness, sheltered or concealed by it, maybe lost in it, was David; and somewhere too, Vicky, Verne and others I'd loved.

In the darkness things always go away from you. Memory holds you down while regret and sorrow kick hell out of you.

The only help you'll get is a few hard drinks and morning.

Chapter Six

I PUSHED THE door open and saw his back bent over the worn mahogany curb of the bar. I sat beside him, ordered a bourbon and told him what I had to.

For a long time then we were both quiet. I could hear traffic sounds from the elevated freeway a block or so away.

"La vie," *he finally said,* "c'est toujours cruelle, n'est-ce-pas?"

"Mais oui," *I said.* "C'est vrai. *And nothing to help us but a few hard drinks and morning.*"

"Le matin, *it is still far away, and this I can do nothing about. But the drinks, I can do. A bottle, please," he said to the bartender, and to me: "You will join me?"*

"Yes," *I said.* "Of course."

And that was it. I skipped a few spaces and typed *The End*, mixed another drink and started proofing the final pages.

Not long after Verne had left, I'd made a pot of coffee, turned on the fans and the stereo, and settled into work. The phone had rung several times and I'd ignored it, letting the machine earn its keep. When the coffee was gone I had mixed a pitcher of martinis and drunk that, then more coffee, more martinis, and about eight in the morning, some scrambled eggs and toast. After that I switched to margaritas, and with the third or fourth came to the end of the novel, far and away the best I'd done, maybe the best I'll ever do. I mailed it off to my agent and slept for three days. Then got up to answer all the calls.

Most of them were junk and hang-ups. One was from Verne giving me her new address. Two were from Janie. The school had called to ask me to fill in for Dr. Palangian, advanced conversational and nineteenth-century French lit, next month while he was in Paris. A magazine editor wondered if I would consider doing a short piece for her, on whatever topic I'd like. The *Times-Picayune* was sending out a book for possible review.

Twice, whoever called neither spoke nor hung up, keeping the line open until the machine automatically closed it. I found those twenty-second segments of tape somehow profoundly unsettling. To this day (for I have them still) I find them so, though without good reason.

I called Janie to tell her what little I'd managed to learn, then Verne to say hello (she wasn't in, so I breathed hard at her machine and told *it* hello instead), then spent the rest of the afternoon on the phone to a few friends and many rank strangers (ticket clerks, a flight steward, cab dispatchers and drivers, hotels, hospitals, hostels) trying to pick up a single loose thread that might ravel back to David.

Nada, as Hemingway said. (A word he later turned into a verb, his last one.)

About eight I knocked off and made some sandwiches and coffee, then read for a while. An hour or so later Dooley, the only detective I know in New York, called back. We were in the service together (myself briefly, him for a couple of hitches) and somehow stayed in touch. He was an MP then.

"Okay, Lew, here it is. I've got a confirmation, David did come in on that plane. The stewardess remembers him because of his manners. Then I've got a hack that remembers him, flashed on the description. Thinks he dropped him midtown, maybe Grand Central or Port Authority. And after that, nothing. Zilch."

"You've been to the apartment?"

"The super told you just the way it is."

"No other leads? Ideas?"

"Short of calling in the crazies with their birch rods and chicken entrails, no. I'm sorry, Lew. I'll put the word out among my contacts here, of course. They're a pretty wide-ranging lot. You never know. One of them might catch sight of him, or hear something, if he's still in the city."

"My thanks, D. I'm expecting a bill."

"For what? I ain't done chickenshit, Lew. I do something, *then* I'll be sending a bill."

"Take care, friend."

"I will. Have to, up here."

I got another follow-up call that night, a few more the next morning, none of them of consequence, buckets full of holes.

Walsh called to say he'd heard about David, let him know if he could do anything to help.

"Verne's gone," I told him.

"Jesus, Lew. Sounds like you reached for your hat and got the chamber pot instead."

And for some reason that cheered me immeasurably.

I walked over to St. Charles and caught the trolley downtown, wandered around Canal and the Quarter like a tourist, stopped off for coffee at Café du Monde and for a brandy at the Napoleon House. Then took in a cheap matinee.

It was a forties-style detective movie, all stark blacks and whites, full of women flaunting cigarettes, silly hats and wisecracks. The hero was a one-time idealist turned mercenary and gone more recently to seed and gin. Ninety minutes later he'd become a solid citizen and, left behind there in movieland when the curtain closed, was probably scouting out real estate just north of town and a few new suits.

It was wonderful.

I walked over to Corondolet in the dark and caught the next trolley, almost empty at first, but it filled quickly as we worked our way around Lee Circle and uptown. A young woman sat in the back alone, looking steadily out the window and crying. The driver kept looking up at her in his mirror.

The house was emptier than I had left it. I mixed a drink and sat in darkness. The news my Cajun had brought the old man in the bar was that his son was dead, needlessly, stupidly dead, and I knew that more than ever before I was writing close to my life, that the old man's bottle and mute acceptance were my own, that I would not see David again. I am not a man much given to the mystic or ineffable, but sitting there that night in the darkness like a cat, with the fruity smell of gin and a murmur of wind from outside, I knew. And I have been right.

Chapter Seven

THE FOLLOWING DAYS are as blurred as that one moment is distinct.

I must have drunk up everything in the house, then gone out for more. I remember walking back along St. Charles with paper bags in both arms, stumbling at a corner but only one of the bottles, miraculously, breaking. Signing a check at a K&B. Walking barefoot on hot sidewalk trying to find my way home and waking the next morning to find the soles of my feet covered with blisters.

A few bright frames, all the rest lost.

At some point Walsh was there (or I thought he was), then Verne and a little later two Indians with a travois. I was a kite floating over crowds that included Janie, David, Robert Johnson, my old man, Verne, Jules Verne, Ma Rainey, Walsh, George Washington Carver, the whole sick crew.

Lots of vintage television. Game shows! Soap operas!

And again one morning woke to pain and thirst, not a rolled *r* anywhere.

It didn't take long this time, a week or so, and I was

turned loose on society once again. I lay around the house drinking endless pots of coffee and reading things like Balzac and Dickens. Taught for Jack Palangian three days a week and had a few good students, started running with a younger member of the French faculty. Did some low-key magazine pieces and a series for the *Times-Picayune* on Cajun culture.

Some nights after work Verne came by and we'd cook, then spend the rest of the evening out on the balcony talking about the old days. "We're just alike that way, Lew," she used to say. "Neither one of us is ever going to have anyone permanent, anyone who'll go the long haul, who cares that much." But she was wrong.

A few months out of hospital, down thirty pounds and a couple of sizes from running, I got galleys for *The Old Man* and finished reading them early one morning (*I pushed the door open and saw his back bent over the worn mahogany curb of the bar*) with tears in my eyes. The book's success some months later surprised me not at all.

And now I must come to some sort of conclusion, I suppose.

I can't imagine what it should be.

I still live in the house Verne and I once lived in together, and she still comes by some nights. I often talk to Vicky, Walsh, Cherie and others. Memory and real voices, and the voices of these characters as I write, fill the rooms. Sometimes regret or sorrow tries to rear up and make itself heard, and sometimes, though not so often as before, I think, it succeeds.

And so, another book. But not about my Cajun this time. About someone I've named Lew Griffin, a man I know both very well and not at all. And I have only to end it now by writing: I went back into the house and wrote. It is midnight. The rain beats at the windows.

It is not midnight. It is not raining.

Continue reading for a preview from the next
Lew Griffin novel

Moth

Chapter One

It was midnight, it was raining.

I scrubbed at the sink as instructed, and went on in. The second set of double doors led into a corridor at the end of which, to the left, a woman sat at a U-shaped desk behind an improvised levee of computers, phones, stacks of paperwork and racks of bound files. She was on the phone, trying simultaneously to talk into it and respond to the youngish man in soiled Nikes and lab coat who stood beside her asking about results of lab tests. Every few moments the phone purred and a new light started blinking on it. The woman herself was not young, forty to fifty, with thinning hair in a teased style out of fashion for at least twenty years. A tag on her yellow polyester jacket read Jo Ellen Heslip. Names are important.

To the right I walked past closetlike rooms filled with steel racks of supplies, an X-ray viewer, satellite pharmacy, long conference tables. Then into the intensive-care nursery, the NICU, itself—like coming out onto a plain. It was half the size of a football field, broken into semidiscrete sections by four-foot tile walls topped with open shelving. (Pods, I'd later learn to call them.) Light flooded in from windows along three walls. The windows were double, sealed: thick outer glass, an enclosed area in which lint and construction debris had settled, inner pane. Pigeons strutted on the sill outside.

Down in the street buses slowed at, then passed, a covered stop. Someone in a hospital gown, impossible to say what sex or age, slept therein on a bench advertising Doctor's Bookstore, getting up from time to time to rummage in the trash barrel alongside, pulling out cans with a swallow or two remaining, a bag of Zapp's chips, a smashed carton from Popeye's.

I found Pod 1 by trial and error and made my way through the grid of incubators, open cribs, radiant warmers: terms I'd come to know in weeks ahead. Looking down at pink and blue tags affixed to these containers.

Baby Girl McTell lay in an incubator in a corner beneath the window. The respirator reared up beside her on its pole like a silver sentinel, whispering: *shhhh, shhhh, shhhh*. LED displays wavered and changed on its face. With each *shhhh*, Baby Girl McTell's tiny body puffed up, and a rack of screens mounted above her to the right also updated: readouts of heart rate, respiration and various internal pressures on a Hewlett-Packard monitor, oxygen saturation on a Nellcor pulse oximeter, levels of CO_2 and O_2 from transcutaneous monitors.

Baby Girl McTell
Born 9/15
Weight 1 lb 5 oz
Mother Alouette

I could hold her in the palm of my hand, easily, I thought. Or could have, if not for this battleship of machinery keeping her afloat, keeping her alive.

The nurse at bedside looked up. Papers lay scattered about on the bedside stand. She was copying from them onto another, larger sheet. She was left-handed, her wrist a winglike curve above the pen.

"Good morning. Would you be the father, by any chance?"

Reddish-blond hair cut short. Wearing scrubs, as they all were. Bright green eyes and a British accent like clear, pure water, sending a stab of pain and longing and loss through me as I thought of Vicky: red hair floating above me when I woke with DT's in Touro Infirmary, Vicky with her Scottish r's, Vicky who had helped me retrieve my life and then gone away.

Teresa Hunt, according to her nametag. But did I really look like an eighteen-year-old's romantic other?

Or maybe she meant the *girl's* father?

I shook my head. "A family friend."

"Well, I had wondered." Words at a level, unaccented. "No one's seen anything of him, as far as I know."

"From what little *I* know, I don't expect you will."

"I see. Well, we are rather accustomed to that, I suppose. Some of the mothers themselves stop coming after a time."

She shuffled papers together and capped her pen, which hung on a cord around her neck. There was print on the side of it: advertising of some sort, drugs probably. Like the notepad Vicky wrote her name and phone number on when I found her at Hotel Dieu.

Tucking everything beneath an oversized clipboard, Teresa Hunt squared it on the stand.

"Look, I'm terribly sorry," she said. "Someone should have explained this to you, but only parents and grandparents are allowed—oh, never mind all that. Bugger the rules. What difference can it possibly make? Is this your first time to see her?"

I nodded.

"And it's the mother you know?"

"Grandmother, really. The baby's mother's mother. We . . . were friends. For a long time."

"I see." She probably did. "And the girl's mother recently died, according to the chart. A stroke, wasn't it?"

"It was."

There was no way I could tell her or anyone else what LaVerne had meant, had been, to me. We were both little more than kids when we met; Verne was a hooker then. Years later she married her doctor and I didn't see her for a while.

When he cut her loose, she started as a volunteer at a rape crisis center and went on to a psychology degree and fulltime counseling. It was a lonely life, I guess, at both ends. And when finally she met a guy named Chip Landrieu and married him, even as I began to realize what I had lost, I was happy for her. For both of them.

"Did she know Alouette was pregnant?"

I shook my head. "Their lives had gone separate ways many years back." So separate that I hadn't even known about Alouette. "She—" Say it, Lew. Go ahead and say her name.

Names are important. "LaVerne had been trying to get back in touch, to find Alouette."

She looked away for a moment. "What's happened to us?"

And in my own head I heard Vicky again, many years ago:

What's wrong with this country, Lew? "Well, never mind all that. Not much we can do about it, is there? Do you understand what's happening here?" Her nod took in the ventilator, monitors, bags of IV medication hanging upside down like transparent bats from silver poles, Baby Girl McTell's impossible ark; perhaps the whole world.

"Not really." Does anyone, I wanted to add.

"Alouette is a habitual drug user. Crack, mainly, according to our H&P and the social worker's notes, but there's a history of drug and alcohol abuse involving many controlled substances, more or less whatever was available, it seems. She makes no attempt to deny this. And because of it, Alouette's baby was profoundly compromised *in utero*. She never developed, and though Alouette did manage to carry her as far as the seventh month, what you're looking at here in the incubator is something more on the order of a five-month embryo. You can see there's almost nothing to her. The eyes are fused, her skin breaks down wherever it's touched, there aren't any lungs to speak of. She's receiving medication which paralyzes her own respiratory efforts, and the machine, the ventilator, does all her breathing. We have her on high pressures and a high rate, and nine hours out of ten we're having to give her hundred-percent oxygen. Two hours out of ten, maybe, we're holding our own."

"You're telling me she's going to die."

"I am. Though of course I'm not supposed to."

"Then why are we doing all this?"

"Because we can. Because we know how. There are sixty available beds in this unit. On any given day, six to ten of those beds will be filled with crack babies like Alouette's. At least ten others are just as sick, for whatever reasons— other kinds of drug and alcohol abuse, congenital disease, poor nutrition, lack of prenatal care. The numbers are climbing every day. When I first came here, there'd be, oh, five to ten babies in this unit. Now there're never fewer than thirty. And there've been times we've had to stack cribs in the hallway out there."

"Are you always this blunt?"

"No. No, I'm not, not really. But we look on all this a bit differently in Britain, you understand. And I think that I may be answering something I see in your face, as well."

"Thank you." I held out a hand. She took it without hesitation or deference, as American women seldom can. "My name is Griffin. Lew."

"Teresa, as you can see. And since Hunt is the name on my nursing license, I use it here. But in real life, away from here, I mostly use my maiden name, McKinney. If there's ever anything I can do, Mr. Griffin, please let me know. This can be terribly hard on a person." She removed vials from a drawer beneath the incubator, checked them against her lists, drew up portions into three separate syringes and injected these one at a time, and slowly, into crooks (called heplocks) in Baby Girl McTell's IV tubing.

There were four IV sites, swaddled in tape. Almost every day one or another of them had to be restarted elsewhere, in her scalp, behind an ankle, wherever they could find a vein that wouldn't blow.

She dropped the syringes into the mouth of a red plastic Sharps container, pulled a sheet of paper from beneath the clipboard and, glancing at a clock on the wall nearby, made several notations.

"I don't know at all why I'm telling you this, Mr. Griffin, but I had a child myself, a son. He was three months early, weighed almost two pounds and lived just over eight days. I was sixteen at the time. And afterwards, because of an infection, I became quite sterile. But it was because of him that I first began thinking about becoming a nurse."

"Call me Lew. Please."

"I don't think the head nurse would care much for that, if she were to hear about it. She's a bit stuffy and proper, you understand."

"But what can one more rule matter? Since, as you say, we've already started breaking them."

"Yes, well, we have done that truly, haven't we, Lew. Do

you think you'd be wanting to speak with one of the doctors? They should be along in just a bit. Or I could try paging one of them."

"Is there anything they can tell me that you can't?"

"Not really, no."

"Then I don't see any reason for bothering them. I'm sure they have plenty to do."

"That they have. Well, I'll just step out for a few minutes and leave the two of you to get acquainted. If you should need anything, Debbie will be watching over my children while I'm gone."

She nodded toward a nurse who sat in a rocking chair across the pod, bottle-feeding one of the babies.

"That's Andrew. He's been with us almost a year now, and we all spoil him just awfully, I'm afraid."

"A year? When will he leave?"

"There's nowhere for him to go. Most of his bowel had to be removed just after birth, and he'll always be needing a lot of care. Feedings every hour, a colostomy to manage. His parents came to see him when the mother was in the hospital, but once she was discharged, we stopped hearing from them.

The police went out to the address we had for them after a bit, but they were long gone. Eventually I suppose he'll be moved upstairs to pediatrics. And somewhere farther along they'll find a nursing home that will take him, perhaps."

I looked from Andrew back to Baby Girl McTell as Teresa walked away. Names are important. Things are what we call them. By naming, we understand. But what name do we have for a baby who's never quite made it into life, who goes on clawing after it, all the while slipping further away, with a focus, a hunger, we can scarcely imagine? What can we call the battles going on here? And how can we ever understand them?

Through the shelves I watched people gather over an Isolette in the next pod. First the baby's own nurse, then another from the pod; next, when one of them went off to get her, a nurse who appeared to be in charge; finally, moments later, the young man in lab coat and Nikes who'd earlier been standing at the desk in front. Various alarms had begun sounding—buzzers, bells, blats—as the young man looked up at the monitors one last time, reached for a transparent green bag at bedside, and said loudly: "Call it."

Overhead, a page started: *Stat to neonatal intensive care, all attendings*. He put a part of the bag over the baby's face and began squeezing it rapidly.

Then I could see no more as workers surrounded the Isolette.

"Sir, I'm afraid I'll have to ask you to step out," Debbie said. She stood and placed Andrew back in his open crib. The child's eyes followed her as she walked away. He didn't cry.

I filed out alongside skittish new fathers, smiling grandparents, a couple of mothers still in hospital gowns and moving slowly, hands pressed flat against their stomachs. An X-ray machine bore down on us through the double doors and lumbered along the hallway, banging walls and scattering linen hampers, trashcans, supply carts. Where's this one? the tech asked. Pod 2, Mrs. Heslip told him.

Most of the others, abuzz with rumor, clustered just outside the doors. Some decided to call it a night and went on to the elevators across the hall, where I knew from experience they'd wait a while. I found stairs at the end of a seemingly deserted hall and went down them (they smelled of stale cigarettes and urine) into the kind of cool, gentle rain we rarely see back in New Orleans. There, when it comes, it comes hard and fast, making sidewalks steam, beating down banana trees and shucking leaves off magnolias, pouring over the edges of roofs and out of gutters that can't handle the sudden deluge.

I turned up the collar of my old tan sportcoat as I stepped out of the hospital doorway just in time to get splashed by a pickup that swerved toward the puddle when it saw me. I heard cackling laughter from inside.

Earlier I had noticed a small café on the corner a few blocks over. Nick's, Rick's, something like that, the whole front of it plate glass, with handwritten ads for specials taped to the glass and an old-style diner's counter. I decided to give it a try and headed that way. Moving through the streets of the rural South I'd fled a long time ago. Bessie Smith had died not too far from here, over around Clarksdale, when the white hospital wouldn't treat her following a car accident and she bled to death on the way to the colored one.

At age sixteen, I had fled. Fled my father's docility and

sudden rages, fled old black men saying "mister" to ten-year old white kids, fled the fields and the tire factory pouring thick black smoke out onto the whole town like a syrup, fled all those faces gouged out and baked hard and dry like the land itself. I had gone to the city, to New Orleans, and made a life of my own, not a life I was especially proud of, but mine nonetheless, and I'd always avoided going back. I'd avoided a lot of things. And now they were all waiting for me.

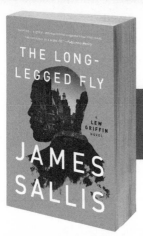
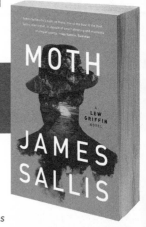

LEW GRIFFIN IS A PRIVATE DETECTIVE, TEACHER, WRITER, POET, AND A BLACK MAN MOVING THROUGH A WHITE MAN'S WORLD. THE DARKEST CORNERS OF NEW ORLEANS ARE ILLUMINATED IN THIS SERIES BY LIVING LEGEND JAMES SALLIS.

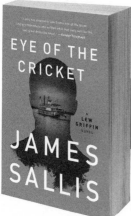

"James Sallis—he's right up there, one of the best of the best."
—Ian Rankin

EYE OF A CRICKET | LEW GRIFFIN, BOOK 4
ISBN: 9781641291491 | EISBN: 9781641291507
11/12/2019 | TRADE PAPERBACK | US $16.95 / CAN $20.95

"One of the most intriguing, disturbing, literate, intelligent novels I've read in years."
—David Bradley

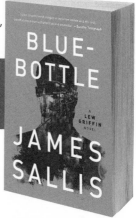

BLUEBOTTLE | LEW GRIFFIN, BOOK 5
ISBN: 9781641291514 | EISBN: 9781641291521
12/03/2019 | TRADE PAPERBACK | US $16.95 / CAN $20.95

"James Sallis is an outstanding crime writer—an outstanding writer period."
—Frances McDormand

GHOST OF A FLEA | LEW GRIFFIN, BOOK 6
ISBN: 9781641291538 | EISBN: 9781641291545
12/03/2019 | TRADE PAPERBACK | US $16.95 / CAN $20.95

"*Ghost of a Flea* bears the marks of a fierce and original writer working at full power."
—Los Angeles Times

Other Titles in the Soho Crime Series

Michael Genelin
(Slovakia)
Siren of the Waters
Dark Dreams
The Magician's Accomplice
Requiem for a Gypsy

Timothy Hallinan
(Thailand)
The Fear Artist
For the Dead
The Hot Countries
Fools' River

(Los Angeles)
Crashed
Little Elvises
The Fame Thief
Herbie's Game
King Maybe
Fields Where They Lay
Nighttown

Mette Ivie Harrison
(Mormon Utah)
The Bishop's Wife
His Right Hand
For Time and All Eternities
Not of This Fold

Mick Herron
(England)
Slow Horses
Dead Lions
Real Tigers
Spook Street
London Rules
Joe Country

Down Cemetery Road
The Last Voice You Hear
Why We Die
Smoke and Whispers

Reconstruction
Nobody Walks
This Is What Happened

Stan Jones
(Alaska)
White Sky, Black Ice
Shaman Pass

Stan Jones cont.
Frozen Sun
Village of the Ghost Bears
Tundra Kill
The Big Empty

**Lene Kaaberbøl &
Agnete Friis**
(Denmark)
The Boy in the Suitcase
Invisible Murder
Death of a Nightingale
The Considerate Killer

Martin Limón
(South Korea)
Jade Lady Burning
Slicky Boys
Buddha's Money
The Door to Bitterness
The Wandering Ghost
G.I. Bones
Mr. Kill
The Joy Brigade
Nightmare Range
The Iron Sickle
The Ville Rat
Ping-Pong Heart
The Nine-Tailed Fox
The Line
GI Confidential

Ed Lin
(Taiwan)
Ghost Month
Incensed
99 Ways to Die

Peter Lovesey
(England)
The Circle
The Headhunters
False Inspector Dew
Rough Cider
On the Edge
The Reaper

(Bath, England)
The Last Detective
Diamond Solitaire
The Summons

Peter Lovesey cont.
Bloodhounds
Upon a Dark Night
The Vault
Diamond Dust
The House Sitter
The Secret Hangman
Skeleton Hill
Stagestruck
Cop to Corpse
The Tooth Tattoo
The Stone Wife
*Down Among
the Dead Men*
Another One Goes Tonight
Beau Death
Killing with Confetti

(London, England)
Wobble to Death
*The Detective Wore
Silk Drawers*
Abracadaver
Mad Hatter's Holiday
The Tick of Death
A Case of Spirits
Swing, Swing Together
Waxwork

Jassy Mackenzie
(South Africa)
Random Violence
Stolen Lives
The Fallen
Pale Horses
Bad Seeds

Sujata Massey
(1920s Bombay)
The Widows of Malabar Hill
The Satapur Moonstone

Francine Mathews
(Nantucket)
Death in the Off-Season
Death in Rough Water
Death in a Mood Indigo
Death in a Cold Hard Light
Death on Nantucket

Seichō Matsumoto
(Japan)
Inspector Imanishi
Investigates

Magdalen Nabb
(Italy)
Death of an Englishman
Death of a Dutchman
Death in Springtime
Death in Autumn
The Marshal and
the Murderer
The Marshal and
the Madwoman
The Marshal's Own Case
The Marshal Makes
His Report
The Marshal
at the Villa Torrini
Property of Blood
Some Bitter Taste
The Innocent
Vita Nuova
The Monster of Florence

Fuminori Nakamura
(Japan)
The Thief
Evil and the Mask
Last Winter, We Parted
The Kingdom
The Boy in the Earth
Cult X

Stuart Neville
(Northern Ireland)
The Ghosts of Belfast
Collusion
Stolen Souls
The Final Silence
Those We Left Behind
So Say the Fallen

(Dublin)
Ratlines

Rebecca Pawel
(1930s Spain)
Death of a Nationalist
Law of Return
The Watcher in the Pine
The Summer Snow

Kwei Quartey
(Ghana)
Murder at Cape
Three Points
Gold of Our Fathers
Death by His Grace

Qiu Xiaolong
(China)
Death of a Red Heroine
A Loyal Character Dancer
When Red Is Black

James Sallis
(New Orleans)
The Long-Legged Fly
Moth
Black Hornet
Eye of the Cricket
Bluebottle
Ghost of a Flea

Sarah Jane

John Straley
(Sitka, Alaska)
The Woman Who
Married a Bear
The Curious Eat Themselves
The Music of What Happens
Death and the Language
of Happiness
The Angels Will Not Care
Cold Water Burning
Baby's First Felony

(Cold Storage, Alaska)
The Big Both Ways
Cold Storage, Alaska

Akimitsu Takagi
(Japan)
The Tattoo Murder Case
Honeymoon to Nowhere
The Informer

Helene Tursten
(Sweden)
Detective Inspector Huss
The Torso
The Glass Devil
Night Rounds
The Golden Calf
The Fire Dance
The Beige Man
The Treacherous Net
Who Watcheth
Protected by the Shadows

Hunting Game

An Elderly Lady Is Up to
No Good

Janwillem van de
Wetering
(Holland)
Outsider in Amsterdam
Tumbleweed
The Corpse on the Dike
Death of a Hawker
The Japanese Corpse
The Blond Baboon
The Maine Massacre
The Mind-Murders
The Streetbird
The Rattle-Rat
Hard Rain
Just a Corpse at Twilight
Hollow-Eyed Angel
The Perfidious Parrot
The Sergeant's Cat:
Collected Stories

Jacqueline Winspear
(1920s England)
Maisie Dobbs
Birds of a Feather